ANDREW V. KUDIN

The Black Suit

- KIEV - UKRAINE -

Power is the goal, and they'll do anything for it.

The Soviet Union is on the verge of collapse. The communist regime is losing control of society. Criminal gangs are fighting for power over the capital of Ukraine. Immerse yourself in a whirlwind of intrigue, betrayals, and moral dilemmas.

When a quiet guy from an intelligent family becomes the leader of one of the most brutal and bloody gangs in the history of modern Ukraine, he is forced to confront some of life's eternal questions. What is love, does it exist? What is more important - pursuing your dreams and knowledge? Or amassing material wealth?

Based on a true story, "The Black Suit" is a riveting, compelling thriller that explores the dark world of Soviet crime, unbridled passion, and patriotism, where the past is the key to understanding the present.

© 2024 Andrew V. Kudin. All rights reserved

ABOUT THE BOOK "THE BLACK SUIT"
(introduction to the English edition)

Today, no one remembers that during the Soviet Union, the topic of organized crime was under a ban. After all, in a country building communism, according to the authorities, there could not be any organized crime.

Before Andrew V. Kudin, no one dared to write on this topic. He was the first.

In 1993, the novel "The Black Suit" was first published in an abridged version (the full version was not allowed by censorship). Despite this, the novel "The Black Suit" was a phenomenal success - 25,000 copies were sold out in a matter of days, and now this edition is a bibliographic rarity.

Many years have passed since then. However, "The Black Suit" is no less attractive than in the early nineties of the last century.

The book is based on actual events. Some of the names in the book are authentic. Most of the characters in the book and their prototypes are no longer alive. There is no censorship, either. This made it possible to publish the book in its full version in its original form with minor author edits in 2023.

"The Black Suit" is a story about love and loneliness against the background of the confrontation between two rival street gangs in the period of severe crisis of Soviet society on the eve of the collapse of the USSR.

The book is interesting from both historical and psychological points of view. The author has devoted many years to studying the psychology of criminals and has a Ph.D. in Law (Research Interests: Criminology) and a Ph.D. in Philosophy and Religious Studies.

Published in English for the first time.

PART I

CHAPTER I

It was late evening. The leaves rustled quietly outside the open window, providing a serene backdrop. A faint, unearthly light in the hallway cast long, wavering shadows on the walls. His wife's voice broke through the silence, her urgent plea echoing in the narrow space, "Don't go," she begged, her eyes filled with a mixture of fear and despair, framed by the kitchen doorway, which was open wide like a portal to an uncertain future.

His slightly trembling fingers frantically tied the laces on his sneakers, each knot trying to anchor itself in the world that seemed to be slipping away.

"It's necessary," he replied with a conviction that didn't match the inner turmoil.

On the dimly lit street across from the entryway stood a sleek BMW, its windows ominously tinted. There were no license plates on the car.

"At this hour?" - she asked a note of incredulity and humility in her voice at the same time.

In a ritualistic motion, he put the car keys in the side pocket of his pants.

"You have a family, kids... Khanya is a scoundrel. Why do you have to go with him?" His wife's words hung in the air, an unspoken plea to come to his senses, to choose the path of safety and responsibility.

He answered with a conviction in which there was a bond that defied condemnation. "Khanya is no scoundrel," he remarked, and there was an unwavering loyalty in his voice. "He is a friend."

He turned away from his wife and took a step toward the exit. There was a quiet click of the lock on the front door. She watched helplessly as the gray shadow of her lover slid into the car with tinted windows.

And then, as if in defiance, the car's headlights flashed, cutting through the darkness like a beacon of doom. The unhappy roar of the engine, like the growl of an untamed beast, blended seamlessly into the evening symphony of Kiev, the city that never sleeps.

***

"In another reality, in another atmosphere, illuminated by an unfamiliar light, the same evening unfolded, with the same palpable tension stamped into the unyielding features of his face.
"I won't be long, you know..."
"I know," came the reply, softly but with deep understanding. Her voice was a soothing balm amidst the impending storm, her words a testament to the unbreakable bond between them.
His eyes, a vast expanse of blue, held her gaze tenaciously, defying the laws of gravity that sought to pull her away. They were eyes that seemed to possess innate wisdom, eyes that witnessed both the ordinary and the extraordinary, eyes that saw everything.
"Best wishes to Khanya for me," the woman said softly. Their gazes converged for a moment in a silent exchange of feelings that spoke volumes.
A nod of the head followed a tacit agreement that required no verbal confirmation. But even as the head nodded, the gaze had already shifted, switched to the uncertain path that lay ahead. It was a poignant moment, a clash of duty and loyalty, responsibility and friendship.
Again, the quiet click of the door echoed in the background, marking a familiar but important turning point. How many times in his life had he heard that sound? It was the sound of parting, the threshold beyond which his joys and sorrows, hopes and fears remained, and never - not once - had it resulted in indifference. That quiet click of the lock on the door was a symbolic reminder that choices in life are often determined by the smallest of actions, and their consequences are felt in the very depths of the heart."

***

At the back of the street was a four-story monolithic building with barred windows, each with a light burning in it. Inside, the officers were bustling about, their movements purposeful but at the same time shrouded in uncertainty. Special Forces, clad in body armor, were preparing for the mission, their hearts beating in unison beneath the protective layer. They had no idea what lay ahead, and orders came from an absent commander who invisibly watched their every step and the synchronized footsteps of their boots echoing down the long corridor.

Light raindrops caressing the dark strands of a soldier's hair added an element of unpredictability to the atmosphere. The street outside the window, quiet and seemingly unremarkable, resembled countless others in the tangled web of Kiev cityscape. Casual passersby quickened their steps, casting wary glances at the long row of cars around which, like shadows at a secret meeting, the conspirators huddled.

A BMW with tinted windows swept swiftly down the winding road, leaving an indelible mark on the otherwise quiet street. Time passed, and the car reappeared at the opposite end of the road, its headlights gradually fading like extinguished stars in the night sky. The sound of closing doors echoed in the air, bringing life back to the once quiet street as if awakening it from a deep sleep.

***

"My God, it's so late! I promised to be home by ten..." Her voice trembled with excitement and guilt as she glanced at the clock, whose hands were inexorably approaching the hour on which the weight of her obligation rested.

A quick, almost apologetic glance escaped from beneath a veil of long dark lashes, revealing a pair of warm, expressive brown eyes. There was a story in those eyes, a mixture of emotions reflected in them - homesickness, anticipation of reprimand, and perhaps a note of defiance that she was caught up in this moment.

The phone was the thin thread connecting her to the world outside this room. With trembling fingers, she twiddled the dial.

"And at home, as bad luck would have it, the line is occupied..." The annoyance of the unforeseen circumstances sounded in her voice as if the universe itself had conspired to keep her from keeping her promise.

From across the room came a soothing voice, softened by the cloud of tobacco smoke that hung in the air.

"You needn't be in a hurry. You can easily catch a cab outside," the voice suggested, and its soothing confidence cut through the tension that hung in the room. "Finish watching the movie, and then go."

On the bedside table beneath the outdated television stood the parents' VCR, a symbol of technological advancement in the restrictive era of the Soviet Union. Surrounding the VCR was a collection of videotapes, each containing foreign films that were not shown in cinemas. Today, in the digital age, VCRs have become a relic, but in the late 80s, they were a valuable possession, available only to those who could afford to buy such expensive equipment.

The television screen went to credit titles, a sign that the movie they were engrossed in was coming to an end. Outside the room, the night thickened, casting a mysterious shroud over the world around them.

In that moment, the room became a microcosm of an era where promises held great meaning, where technology was a luxury, and the night concealed both the ordinary and the extraordinary.

***

Two rows of parked cars stood on both sides of the street, forming a corridor that seemed to converge at the very center of the city thoroughfare. In the center of this corridor, a group of people gathered under a lone streetlight glowing faintly among the branches of overhanging trees.

"What do you want?" The words hung in the air.

Raindrops clung to strands of dark hair, but they could be shaken off by tilting the head back, a physical manifestation of the tension that permeated the night.

"You stuck your nose where it didn't belong, Khanya," he replied. There was hard determination in his voice. "Your people are trading on my land. If they are trading, they must pay."

"Who gave you the right to decide where I can and cannot go?" There was anger in Khanya's voice. "This city does not belong to you. Go back to the Caucasus and divide the land there as you like!"

The headlights of approaching cars pierced the night, illuminating the scene of the confrontation. The people standing on the road moved toward the sidewalk, where the spreading branches of chestnut trees stretched out, creating a bizarre pattern of shadows dancing on the walls of nearby buildings. The shadows, merging into amorphous figures, painted a mysterious tapestry on the city's canvas.

"Why do we talk to him?" - muttered one of Ahmed's heavyset guards with a note of contempt. "Men like him used to crawl on their knees in front of us."

Khanya calmly shifted his gaze to Ahmed's sturdy build, a powerhouse whose appearance spoke more of brawn and muscle than grace. The gnawed ears, short nose, and empty clear eyes created a portrait of pathetic humanity.

"You want a war?" Ahmed's words, spoken with a cold, commanding tone, broke through the tension. "Khanya, my decision remains unchanged. You are too young to meddle in my affairs."

Confrontation hung in the air like a storm cloud. In the middle of the cityscape, under the flickering streetlights, two street gangs clashed with words sharper than any weapon.

***

The sharp ringing of the telephone shattered the silence in the hallway. "Lali? Hey. What are you up to? Oh... Your guy hasn't called? I'm so tired of their late-night escapades! Are they supposed to be here soon? Who knows... I've been alone all this time. Can I come over?"
A melodic tone pierced the quiet of the foyer. A slender brunette clad in a short robe, disengaged the door chain and swung open the door.
"Hello, Lali," she greeted.
Behind her best friend stood two unfamiliar men.

***

Which is more dangerous - a towering avenue with the cacophonous roar of crowds or unremarkable streets that quietly beckon? Calm, inconspicuous streets create the illusion of safety. Calm reasoning holds back heated emotions.
"Why bother each other?" Standing to Khanya's right, a man in a rough wool sweater pronounced in a sweet cat-like voice.
"Life in the underworld is hard. We all know that" the man continued. "But there aren't that many of us, and the city is huge. There's room for everyone here."
The man in the sweater and Ahmed were about the same age, both in their early forties. They were of sturdy build and exuded outward calmness. However, they were not standing side by side but opposite each other.
"Let's think it over and find a compromise. You'll see the conflict will dissolve by itself. By the way, you mentioned war. You can

rest assured that there will be no winners in it. Everyone will lose - some more, some less... So don't have any illusions. "

***

Her long, disheveled black hair scattered haphazardly across the white sheets like a chaotic river of darkness, a stark contrast to the cleanliness of the linens. Her lifeless eyes were frozen with calm and fear.
Soft, fluttering curtains framed the window, allowing pale light to filter in. It fell softly on her face, casting an unreal glow on it. The walls, painted in the softest shade of lavender, whispered of serenity, but at the same time, the atmosphere was heavy and unspoken.
The silence was broken by two male voices.
The first voice, rough and unyielding, remarked with a touch of regret, "She looks like an angel."
The second voice, softer, with a tinge of weariness, indifferently replied, "She was worse than a beast."
The whole world seemed to hold its breath, becoming an unwilling participant in this grim scene. The contrast between her vulnerability and the harshness of her lifeless gaze created a poignant picture. The weight of judgment and the echoes of a painful past seemed to hang in the air, creating an atmosphere of tension and unresolved questions.

***

The movie came to an end, and the videocassette recorder blinked with mild surprise, obediently displaying the day of the week and the time. The home phone, however, remained unanswered; the phone line was still busy. A palpable tension hung in the room.
"There's sure to be a storm waiting for me at home! I completely forgot to tell my parents of my late return," exclaimed one of the girls, her voice trembling with excitement. The exigency of the

situation made them descend the stairs rapidly, each step recoiling with gravity. In a minute or two, they would be out on the street to hail a cab.

***

"Khanya, I hope we won't have to meet again?"
"Who knows," Khanya replied with enigmatic confidence. "One thing I can promise is that everything will work out for the best."
As the car headlights flashed, their intersecting beams cast restless shadows that scattered and took refuge among the waiting vehicles.

***

"I'd crush that scoundrel," Ahmed seethed with anger. It was only now, as he settled into his car after the negotiations, that he allowed his emotions to surface.
"Did you see how they tucked their tails?" one of the wrestlers on the back seat chimed in deferentially.
The maroon Honda merged onto Paton Bridge.
"Tonight, you'll give the police chief a call," Ahmed casually tossed out to the stout man at the wheel.
"Thank him for the backup. And pass on that I haven't forgotten his request."

***

On the passenger seat behind Khanya sat a nervous passenger and looked anxiously at the road ahead. The interior of the car was soft with the soft sounds of music.
"You're going to kill us with this kind of driving! We're going home, not to the cemetery!"
The car jumped out into the oncoming lane of the road and nearly hit a truck traveling toward it.

"Slow down, Rakhit!" Khanya ordered briefly, keeping his eyes on the scenery passing by.

The speedometer arrow slowly drifted to the left as the car slowed down. The passenger in the back seat relaxed and carelessly reached into his pocket for a cigarette.

***

A short telephone conversation.

A contented, burly man drank a shot of Armenian cognac and went to bed. His footsteps felt the heavy satisfaction of intoxication.

At the other end of the wire, a stout man sat at the kitchen table. He was not even fifty, but the weight of the experience had etched wrinkles into his face, making him seem much older. His police uniform lay carelessly abandoned in the hallway. There were puffs of cigarette smoke in the air. His movements, reminiscent of military precision, contrasted sharply with the fear bubbling in his veins, like streams of cigarette smoke rising to the ceiling.

A four-story building. Iron bars on the windows, tired men behind them, waiving their guns and body armor. Today, they didn't need to take them to the streets to defend the law. Tomorrow, or maybe in a few days, they will put on their body armor again - the cycle of law and order. For most of them, this routine is the essence of their existence. But they were just puppets, and puppets are not supposed to think about who is pulling their strings.

***

An ordinary apartment building on the left bank of the Dnieper. The entrance was a bit dirty, and the stairwell had not been cleaned for a long time. In his time, Akhmed had made a lot of effort to make sure that friends, not random strangers, lived next door to his apartment. So, at least in his own home, he had no cause for concern. Still, his animal instincts told him to remain vigilant. Instead of brushing off Manyunya, who lived a floor above,

Ahmed entered the apartment with him, as he usually did. They checked both rooms, then the bedroom. The floor lamp next to the bed was lit, casting a pale light on a crystal vase of artificial flowers. Lali was asleep, with her face turned away to the wall.
Ahmed turned on the lights in the bathroom, kitchen, and toilet. Manyunya, rubbing his short nose impatiently, fussed at the doorstep. Ahmed had become overly suspicious of everything lately, and it often got on his nerves.
"Is something wrong?" - Manyunya asked.
"We're going to the market tomorrow. Don't oversleep," replied Ahmed.
The door closed behind Manyunya with a creak. Ahmed stopped at the entrance to the bedroom, unbuttoned his pants, and walked over to the bed. He found the position of Lali's body and her immobility strange. Ahmed approached the bed to examine the girl. Suddenly, as if from a powerful electric shock, he convulsively collapsed on his back, unable to utter a word from the excruciating pain. Someone hastily pulled a plastic tablecloth under him to avoid staining the carpet with blood.
Two voices sounded above Ahmed.
The first voice trembled, though it was rough and firm: "I envy your nerves. I could never do that..."
The second voice was soft and tired, "At the end of their conversation, Khanya had to promise Ahmed that everything would work out for the best".

***

"You have no idea how much trouble I'm going to be in!" Brown eyes blinked with a tinge of resentment.
The girls tried to hail a cab on the deserted street, but there was no one in sight, and no cars were passing by. Suddenly, a BMW with tinted windows popped out from around the corner and stopped. Then, it slowly reversed.

"Where to go, girls?" asked the guy sitting next to the driver.

"Nowhere," the brown-haired girl replied without taking her eyes off the road.

"My friend doesn't get in the car with strangers. Besides, you're not a cab," the second girl said deliberately loudly, eyeing the brunet with interest. The guy behind the wheel grinned, catching her gaze.

"Don't we know each other? No? That's odd. After all, we live in the same town..."

There was a slight pause. An appraising glance ran down the girl's legs, then a nod toward the driver.

"She needs Lesnaya Street," the brown-eyed friend gestured.

The back door obediently swung open. An unspoken question hung in the air, "To go or not to go?"

"Go," the girl said deliberately loudly. "If they just try to insult you, we'll figure them out quickly by numbers."

After a moment of hesitation, the girl got into the car and whispered: "Goodbye." The BMW sped forward. Her friend looked at them with bewilderment, muttering to herself: "A car without license plates. How strange..."

***

The left bank of the Dnipro River. Streetlights were shattered, but they were not particularly needed. The sky was clear, and the night was bright. It was an incredibly quiet place, seldom frequented by casual passersby.

From the sixth floor, ropes were lowered. Two bags silently slid down and were carefully caught by someone's hands. Following them, two silhouettes, one after the other, glided through the air. Another moment and the ropes fell to the ground.

***

Under the bridge near the metro station, a traffic police officer signaled the car with tinted windows to stop. The car slowed down. A long, skinny arm holding a crumpled bill appeared from the open window.
"ID?" - The policeman asked.
"Piss off!" - followed the defiant reply.
The BMW quickly fled the scene. The traffic police officer hesitated, looking at the money in his hand. Then he nonchalantly tucked it into his pocket and returned to the patrol car.
"Will there ever come a time when I no longer encounter policemen on my way?" - Rakhit sighed, sitting down in the driver's seat and shaking his head.
The speedometer arrow moved steadily to the right as the car turned.
"Do you talk to everyone so rudely?" The brown-eyed girl asked from the back seat, watching the two men in front curiously.
"He had an unhappy childhood," replied Khanya, turning to the girl.
"What is there to talk about with policemen? Cops are like rats on the road looking for profit. No self-respecting man would wear that lousy uniform," Rakhit added.
"Don't be so quick to judge. There are different types of people in the police force like everywhere else."
Long brown hair cascaded down to her waist, short skirt, and slender legs. Khanya frankly regarded the girl and slowly, unnoticed, ran his hand over the back of the car seat as if it were the girl's back.
"Someone who constantly digs through trash will inevitably end up in the dirt," Khanya said with a smirk.
"This is my house!" - The girl interrupted the guy.
After circling the flowerbed, the BMW stopped near a row of pay phones.

"Take it," the girl offered the money, this time in a softer tone.
"Charming fingers," the brown-haired man's gaze slid down her outstretched hand.
"That won't do," the driver smirked.
Instead of three rubles, five appeared. The thin lips were tightly compressed.
"Is that enough?"
"Put the money away," Khanya said calmly, ignoring the money in her outstretched hand. "Instead of money, please give me your phone number."
"I don't give my number to anyone. Besides, I never get acquainted with people on the street. Take it!"
The money clutched between her fingers hung in the air.
"Then let's get acquainted," Khanya continued nonchalantly, ignoring the money in her outstretched hand.
"I'm busy."
"All day?"
"Until six."
"Let's meet at seven."
"Where?"
"Maybe in the city center? For example, at the entrance to Khreshchatyk metro station."
"I may not come."
"Are you always so ruthless?"
"Bye."
The frail figure disappeared in the shade of the trees. Rakhit's left hand rested on the steering wheel.
"She won't come," Rakhit said.
"She will come," Khanya replied firmly. "You can be sure of that."

***

The streets of the city sink gently into the night, enclosing themselves in its embrace. Silence and tranquility envelop the houses, the spring warmth gently penetrating the open window, caressing her brown hair. Brown eyes gaze up at the stars, getting lost in their distant twinkle. "He's kind and very charming. But a little rough," she thought with a hint of sadness. Regret lurked in her heart at the thought that she might never see this guy again. Slowly, her eyelashes lowered, carrying the girl's thoughts away on the wings of desire.

In that quiet moment, a whirlwind of emotions rushes through her mind, weaving a tapestry of memories and dreams. She longs to see him again, to feel the warmth of his presence and hear his voice. But, alas, fate had decreed otherwise, and she let the night carry her, and her heart carry the weight of longing and the weight of unspoken words.

***

"Do you need me anymore today?"
"No. Let's meet tomorrow."
Without waiting for the elevator, Khanya briskly climbed to the third floor. He paused in the stairwell. A metallic cabinet on thick cables buzzed past him. Khanya always took the stairs to his floor and never used the elevator. The elevator reminded him of a trap that could stop between floors at the most inconvenient moment.
Entering his apartment, he heard the phone ringing. From somewhere far away, as if from the depths of the underworld, a voice reached him - soft, weary:
"It's done, Khanya. You don't need to worry."
Above the writing desk hung an icon. The powerful, authoritative gaze of black eyes met the gentle gaze of Christ.
"Forgive me, Lord..."

CHAPTER II

The countenances of the streets, like the weary faces of budget-conscious train station prostitutes, held an eerie resemblance. Superficially diverse, yet fundamentally sharing a worn and weathered quality. It's a curious parallel that unveils itself when one delves deep into the transformation that time, much like an artist's brushstroke, bestows upon both the streets and the people who walk on them.

Years later, those relentless sculptors of existence mold the visage of the urban landscape just as they etch lines and stories into human faces. Consider for a moment the iconic Khreshchatyk, often referred to as the heartbeat of Ukraine, and contemplate how it might one day metamorphose into a serene, garden-like boulevard akin to the alluring images presented in glossy travel brochures. This grand avenue, with its bustling shops, lively cafes, and throngs of people, was a chameleon, forever shifting in response to the tides of time.

Yet, for all its potential to evolve, in May of 1990, Khreshchatyk remained far removed from the tranquil, picturesque vision many had hoped for. It was a street in the throes of its own identity crisis, caught between the dreams of its citizens and the weight of its history. The daytime hours brought a frenzy of activity as the behemoth city's four million inhabitants hustled and bustled through their lives, leaving behind a trail of dreams and aspirations. But as twilight descended, a transformation unfolded. What had not been fully processed during the day in the immense digestive tract of the metropolis was regurgitated onto Khreshchatyk's cobblestone pavements.

The remnants of a day's worth of toil and turmoil painted an intriguing tapestry of urban life. Discarded newspapers rustled in the breeze, a testament to the city's constant thirst for news and information. The lingering aroma of street food vendors competed with the scents of blooming flowers, weaving a complex olfactory narrative unique to Khreshchatyk in the evenings. Neon signs flickered to life, casting a kaleidoscope of colors upon the sea of humanity navigating the streets, each individual a character in their own story, briefly intersecting with others in the grand drama of city life.

So there it was, in the twilight hours, that the true essence of Khreshchatyk was revealed—a living, breathing organism pulsating with the collective energy, dreams, and desires of its inhabitants. A paradoxical blend of chaos and beauty, it was a testament to the enduring spirit of a city that refused to be defined by the whims of time or the confines of expectations.

***

Six electronic chimes echoed over the central district of the city in a deep, long echo. Khanya took his time getting out of the car, looking around lazily. In his hands, he held a bouquet of flowers. Each petal seemed to hold a secret, a message waiting to be revealed, but one thing was certain: something special was going to happen today. This fragile girl, whom he had been looking forward to seeing, had touched something in the depths of his soul. She was not like all the others. There was something special, mysterious, and elusive in the depths of her brown eyes.

Khanya's footsteps echoed softly as he walked down the sidewalk, the pulse of the city beating in the background. His contemplative gaze took in the details of the cityscape as if rediscovering a familiar place.

***

Two richly dressed guys from Akhmed's entourage approached Khreshchatyk metro station from the direction of the central grocery store.

"Look - Khanya!"

One of the guys slowed down and slung his bag over his right shoulder. Inside, vodka bottles rang resentfully.
"Indeed. Alone, with flowers..."
"Maybe for a funeral?"
The buddy laughed.
"I wonder who he's going to see?"
A brown-eyed girl came out of the metro. A slender figure in a short skirt and a tight-fitting blouse walked gracefully and easily on high heels toward a broad-shouldered man in a black shirt. The guy with the bag stared unceremoniously at the girl's feet. His buddy sighed enviously:
"Juvenile. Seventeen years old, no more..."
"Uh-huh."
"I'd like to fuck her too..."
"Yeah."

***

A sweet smile. A mischievous glance.
"Hello. Am I late? Oh, is this for me?" Her petite nose nestled into the white roses. "Actually, I didn't think I would come..."
The girl took the young man by the arm, and they began to stroll slowly along Khreshchatyk. Two pairs of eyes watched them from behind.
"You said he was alone. Khanya never walks alone."

***

"Excuse me. May I interrupt your conversation?"
The bar. A narrow, stuffy room. Quiet music was playing in the background. An unshaven man leaned on a table.
"Sorry, I'll leave you alone for a moment..."
Khanya rose from the table.
The brown-eyed girl looked at the man in his forties who called out to her boyfriend. He was dressed in a coarse-knit gray sweater,

jeans, and white sneakers. From beneath thick wheat-colored eyebrows, a quick look of small eyes stared back at him.
Khanya turned back to the girl.
"Sorry, I left you for a few minutes. I had to have a word with an old friend."
"You have so many friends."
"One can never have too many friends."
A light clink of glasses clinking together.
"Do you want me to be drunk?"
"A bottle of champagne?"
Laughter.
"You didn't even tell me your name."
"Really? I'm terribly shy."
"What's the name of a terribly shy person?"
"Oleg."
"I'm Violetta."
"A very pretty but very long name. And what were you called as a child?"
"Exactly the same as it is now. Only without the first syllable - Lettochka, Letta."

***

Parallel to the high-speed tramline, a black Volga car sped along. Korotyshka nervously shifted in the back seat.
"Are you sure we won't have any trouble because of that bitch?"
The "bitch" in question was a twenty-year-old college student majoring in economics who supplemented her income by engaging in prostitution. Her services were utilized by both the occupants of the black Volga car and the people they were en route to see.

***

Violetta absentmindedly glanced at her watch.

"Are you in a hurry?"
"Why do you think so?"
"Your gaze..."
"It's just a habit."
The girl's fingers timidly brushed against her companion's hand.
***

At the sight of the man in the rough-knit sweater, the owner's face blurred into a grin, revealing jagged teeth. Behind him, breathing hoarsely, Korotyshka was tapping his feet on the floor.
"Punctuality is a trait of businessmen," the guest in the gray sweater remarked, sinking down on the couch and seemingly without interest as he looked around the apartment.
Low ceilings. Adjoining rooms. A Persian rug hung on the wall, with a "Declaration of Human Rights" cut out of a newspaper pinned to it. The guest's attention was drawn to the owner of the apartment, a self-assured, unshaven man in his thirties.
"You're not alone?"
He grinned. "Just some old classmates happened to drop by."
A bulky and cumbersome cube-shaped "elephant" emerged from the kitchen. A quick glance was enough to realize that they couldn't be classmates because of the age difference. Korotyshka wheezed even louder.
"They just came in for a beer... You can trust these guys. You can talk freely in their presence."
"Do you allow it?" - the man in the sweater asked somewhat strangely. "In that case, show me the gun."
"Show me the money first."
"How can we do without money?"
The man in the sweater opened a blue bag. Inside were wads of money.
"Yes, of course," the round-faced man fussed, moving from room to room. The "classmates" settled languidly in the chairs opposite the couch.

"Our mutual acquaintance wouldn't dare introduce me to unreliable people, would she? By the way, how long have you known her?"

The man shrugged indifferently. "Before she started using drugs, her face seemed a little more attractive to me."

The man with round eyes grinned. "Really? Well, she looks pretty good now, too.... Here, all eleven of them. Thirty rounds each."

There were brand-new revolvers lying on the floor. The man bent over them. "There should have been twelve in all. It turns out that one of the three has a loaded gun in his pocket. More likely, two of them. The one in the white T-shirt is too timid. He won't be able to fire a shot, much less scare anyone properly."

"I wouldn't take any of that stuff with me."

"Was it hard to get the goods through customs?"

"There's no customs for good guys."

"We should go to the woods or the suburbs to check the goods."

The smiles disappeared. The seller's voice took on a metallic tinge. "The guns are in excellent condition. You can say it's straight from the store. That's easy to check. Either you buy them, or we give the goods to other customers. No one goes to the woods or the outskirts."

The distant sounds of the city continued to echo outside the walls of the apartment. Inside the apartment, time stretched too slowly. As the tension grew, the room seemed to close in on itself, turning the once cozy apartment into a pressure cooker of uncertainty. The round-eyed man's face betrayed his growing anxiety, beads of sweat beading on his forehead and his fingers twitching slightly.

In contrast, the man in the gray sweater radiated a disturbing calmness, his steely gaze fixed on every person in the room as if assessing all their thoughts and intentions.

The man in the sweater smiled kindly.

"Okay, that fits. How much do we owe you?"

The salesman obligingly lowered his voice: "As we agreed - eleven at two hundred and three hundred each. Total twenty-five thousand three hundred rubles."
"For the sake of simplicity and friendship, it wouldn't hurt to round it up to twenty-five thousand."
"Just for the sake of friendship..."
A wad of money in a bank wrapper appeared from the bag.
The "classmates" sitting in the chairs visibly relaxed. Following the money, a small black object with the safety off appeared in the buyer's hand, seemingly out of nowhere. His index finger rested on the trigger.
"Don't move. Nine grams of lead can calm down overly nervous people."
Wiping the sweat from his forehead, Korotyshka quickly transferred the goods into a blue gym bag. The salesman's glasses fogged up. "Classmates" blinked in surprise. Everything happened so quickly that they did not have time to realize what was happening. Shorty jumped out onto the landing and ran down the stairs. "Take it easy," the man in the sweater whispered friendly in his ear from behind.
The engine of the black Volga rumbled quietly.
Five minutes passed, then ten... Nothing disturbed the tranquility of the quiet, unassuming street, one of the hundreds of such streets in Kiev.

***

A man in a plain gray sweater walked into the bar and approached Khanya's table.
"Having a relax?" - He asked.
Khanya looked up at the man questioningly.
"We're leaving soon. Are you staying?" - He inquired.
"I have nothing to do here," the man replied.

"Shall we go, then?" - Khanya turned to the girl. Violetta nodded in agreement. Khanya stood up, and they headed towards the exit together. Violetta walked in front. Khanya was half a step behind. Without turning his head, he asked the man in the gray sweater, "What do you say?" he said.
"Nobody moved," the man replied.
"Call this number," Khanya said, discreetly passing a slip of paper with a phone number from hand to hand to the man in the gray sweater.
"You deliver the goods at twenty. Then you find Fix. You'll convert my twenty-five percent into dollars at a ratio of one to fifteen."
"Will he agree?"
"Would he have a choice?"
"When do I meet you?" the man in the sweater asked.
"I'll find you myself."
The man in the gray sweater slowed his step, and his figure disappeared into the bustle of the city as if he had never been there.

***

Standing in the hallway, Letta looked at the interior of the apartment with curiosity.
"I never realized there were apartments with such a convenient layout," she remarked.
Khanya helped her take off her shoes. "It used to be a three-room apartment. I didn't need three rooms since I live alone. Friends helped renovate it and turned it into a two-bedroom. It's gotten more spacious..."
"I hadn't heard that such remodeling was allowed," Letta remarked.
"We didn't ask permission," Khanya replied.
"May I come in?"
"Of course. Coffee or wine?"

"Coffee."

Violetta entered the living room. There was a huge, thick Persian rug on the floor. An oak desk with many drawers stood. Above the desk hung an icon.

"You have so many books!"

The girl said with admiration.

The bookcases stretched from floor to ceiling. Khanin put the tray on the desk.

"Books are like people - you can talk to them, argue with them, but they are better than people." - Khanya sat down on the carpet. – "Books often reflect the best part of human nature. The worst remains in bodies."

The girl sat down on the couch next to the guy.

"You don't like people?"

"What does it mean to love? There are too many animals roaming the streets of cities."

"Animals? I don't understand..."

Khanya thought about it:

"Imagine - you're walking down the street, politely giving way to everyone. But sooner or later, someone roughly pushes you in the back with his shoulder. Just like that. Just because you're walking down the same street as him. What then? Humiliatedly step aside, giving way?"

"You're a strong man. You have the generosity to forgive."

Khanya lightly touched the girl's thighs, the sensation as gentle as an artist's brushstroke on a canvas. Then he leaned forward and slowly parted the girl's tantalizing lips with the soft tip of his tongue...

His eyes looked at her as if she were everything in the world to him, his eyes glistening with arousal, reflecting her beauty. His hands trembled slightly as he took her by the waist, pulling her close to him. He slowly drank the pleasure from her lips as if afraid of ruining the magic of this moment. It was a kiss filled with passion and tenderness, a kiss that was impossible to forget.

His heart was beating so hard she could hear every beat of it. She felt his hands touch her breasts.

The girl softly slapped the man's hand away.

"You're in a hurry..."

Violetta shuddered as she felt the touch of his hands beneath her clothing. A wave of pleasure akin to madness swept over her. Violetta had often imagined how it would happen, but she hadn't expected it to happen so quickly. In an unfamiliar apartment and with a man she had seen for only the second time in her life. Was Khanya the desirable fellow from her fairy tale dreams? Or was it just an illusion? The world in the imagination and the real world are fundamentally different things.

Cradling the man's head against her naked chest, Violetta sank onto her back, bending her legs at the knees.

Clothes are scattered in disorder on the floor.

A quiet, sweet moan escaped her lips. A moan filled with pain and pleasure. He entered her, and she moved towards him, allowing him to penetrate her deeper and deeper. The air was saturated with the intoxicating smell of sweat and perfume, a heady cocktail that only heightened the senses.

Their bodies moved in a rhythm as old as time itself.

Outside the window, there was a cloudless, huge night sky, the depth of which was incomprehensible. Under the sky hung the alarming silence of a tired evening city shrouded in stillness and fatigue.

CHAPTER III

Her gaze fell on the clock. Seven in the morning. A wide antique bed. A huge, massive closet in the corner, obviously filled with clothes. The thought of seeing her parents kept her awake. For the first time in her life, Violetta was sleeping in someone else's house. Sitting on the edge of the bed, the girl lowered her feet onto the soft, fluffy carpet. The mirror reflected her luxurious brown hair, firm, slender body, and thousands of folds of crumpled bedclothes. Violetta tiptoed out into the hallway and peered into the next room. Khanya was sitting at the table in a dark red plaid shirt, carelessly thrown over his naked body, writing something quickly on a piece of paper. Every two or three minutes, the phone rang. A few short phrases. Silence. The phone rang again:
"I'm listening. Yes. Is everything in place? When? Write down the phone..."
Silence again.
Violetta quietly approached him from behind and gently wrapped her arms around his strong shoulders.
Khanya wrapped his whole body around her and pulled her to him, kissing her moist, hot lips with pleasure.
"Oleg, my parents will kick me out of the house. What should I do then?"
"I'll rent an apartment for you."
"You won't take me in?"
"I'll come to you every day."
"You're lying. You'll get bored of me and leave me."
"Silly."
A loud sigh in return.
"I have to go home."
"The car is parked under the house."
"I guess so. You'd do anything to get rid of me!"
The girl took a slender, teasing gait and headed for the shower.

***

Eight o'clock in the morning. The girl strode out of the entryway. Khanya followed her with his hands in the pockets of his black jeans. The pale spring sun was hidden behind the clouds, casting a dim glare on the dark windows of the houses. Violetta stopped.
"Where did he come from?"
Rakhit was dozing in the BMW with the tinted windows.
"The car was waiting for you in the driveway the whole time."
"I thought you were joking. Did Yura wait for us all night?"

***

Eight in the morning. Crimea. Double room in the hotel "Yalta". There are two voices in the room.
The first one is rough and harsh:
"If only you knew how bad I feel!"
The second voice is soft and tired:
"What could make you feel good? The vodka you drank all night, or the street hookers to whom you poured out your soul until morning? Pull yourself back together. Otherwise, you'll be in trouble."

***

Nine thirty in the morning. Kiev. A mute reproach in her father's tired eyes. The sleepless night, the dried tears on her mother's face. Lowering her head, Violetta walked silently to her room.

***

Ten o'clock in the morning. There come the first signs of life in the cafe. Judging by the light odor, something was being cooked, fried, and put on plates in the basement. Opposite the cafe, on the front seat of a black Volga, Korotyshka was sniffing and squirming loudly.

"Gosha! Him!"

At the far end of the street loomed a sleepy, big man with broken ears.

"How many times have I taught you: don't yell. He's him."

The man walked leisurely toward the wrestler. At the sight of forty-year-old Gosha in a gray knitted sweater, the hundred-pound man drew in the air with his nostrils in an animal-like manner, turned his head, and stopped. A streetcar slowly passed down the street, and passers-by glimmered in the store windows. An ordinary street on an ordinary day.

Two stubby teenagers in school uniforms came out of a nearby alley. As they passed the big man, one of them suddenly stopped and, with all his might, brought the steel pipe down on the back of the wrestler's head. The blow was not precise but strong. Groaning, the guy grabbed his head with his hands and turned around sharply. The second teenager cautiously ran in from the other side and took more careful aim. He calmly delivered the blow, putting all his strength into it. Blood spurted from the man's flattened nose.

"Help! Police!" - an elderly woman with a poodle suddenly shouted when she saw schoolboys beating up an athlete.

"Call an ambulance!" - shouted an intelligent man in a cheap Chernigov-made suit, who had already joined the crowd of onlookers around the wrestler, who was stretched out on the pavement.

Next to the fellow lying on the ground squatted a tall forty-year-old man in a gray sweater. Small eyes under wheat-colored eyebrows crossed the wrestler's dull, pain-filled eyes. "That's how it is - you live, breathe oxygen, walk here and there, and suddenly, on a crowded street, you're sent for treatment at your own paycheck. Next time, they'll probably kill you if you mess around."

The ambulance arrived surprisingly quickly. The crowd of spectators grew more and more, but the man in the gray knit sweater was no longer among them.

***

A quarter past ten. Cafe. Semi-basement. The disgruntled face of a waitress or a whore:
"We're not working!"
A short, stout man in a white T-shirt with an American flag and the inscription "Perestroika" was standing in front of her.
"We're not here to eat."
"Where is Senia?" - A man in a gray knit sweater asked, entering the hall.
"Semion Davydovich! Here to see you!" - squeaked the girl hysterically, looking into the back room.
The gray-haired, solid Jew with no less solid belly did not keep them waiting long.
"What do you want?" - His voice sounded irritated.
"To teach you how to speak politely to visitors. Set the table, fucker, if you don't want me to explain obvious things to you when my stomach is empty."
Semion Davidovich, wiping drops of sweat from his forehead, hurried to the telephone set. Frantically dialed a familiar number. One, another... Akhmed's phone was silent.

***

It was two o'clock in the afternoon. Everything around was imbued with a labor rhythm reflecting the industrial character of the area. The powerful walls of the Bolshevik factory, the elegant symbol of the city's production capacity, rose not far from the subway. The rhythm of the factory matched the pace of life in the neighborhood. In one such area, always full of life and movement, a group of energetic young men gathered. Their actions aroused the interest of onlookers around them. Casual passers-by joined them, too. The men were playing "thimbles," a simple game that at first sight seemed so innocent and simple to the untrained observer. But only those in the know realized that this game was not so much about luck as it was about dexterity and the ability to deceive.

Deception, however, was at the heart of these amusements. If you guessed which way the ball hid from the thimbles, you could become richer - the money at stake would go to you. But if you were wrong, you had to walk away with sadness in your eyes and empty pockets - and that was what happened most of the time.

It was one of those games where victory was predetermined in advance, and casual passers-by had no chance of success. Everything was planned out so that they would inevitably lose. People hoped for luck but left disappointed, having lost their money. It was a game in which only those who controlled the rules won.

The fellows from Akhmed's gang had spotted the guy in the dark red plaid shirt from afar. A tall blond man leaned over the thimble-twirling Avar.

"Hasan, Khanya is coming here."

"Let him come."

The game continued. Another player from among the casual passers-by went home without a gold wedding ring. Khanya stopped near an elderly woman carrying a shopping bag. Three thieves in their twenties walked behind him, arms defiantly crossed over their chests. One minute, two, three ... The Avar stopped abruptly. The caps froze. The black ball rolled lazily on the cardboard board.

"What are you staring at, like a gopher for profit? - The rough voice of a man who knew his worth. Rough facial features.

Two pairs of black eyes met under the curious gazes of gawkers and passers-by.

"If I am a gopher, then what are you?"

The crowd fell silent.
"I'm the one who crushes gophers," - Hasan said harshly.
"Get out of here." - The blond man's voice came from behind.
Khanya smiled kindly:
"'You know I never argue with those who are stronger than me,"- he said calmly, stepping aside.
"Catch him?" - A question in the blond man's eyes.
Hassan remained silent. A graceful brown-haired man in a snow-white shirt was waiting for Khanya forty paces away.
"Vladik, do we need animals that specialize in crushing gophers?"
Three or four cars pulled up to the sidewalk.
"Predators, or what?"
A cigarette butt flew into the nearest trash can.
"Looks like that."
"This side or the other side of the barricade?"
"The other side."
"I guess no."
"How will they figure it out?"
"You'll see it."
A sharp command in a husky voice. Tough guys with sticks and chains jumped out of the cars. A scream. Someone stumbled and fell. The crowd of onlookers dispersed in a flash. One of the thieves ran away. Someone grabbed the tall blond man's hair and hit his face against his knee. Resting his hands on the sidewalk, the Avar spat out his teeth with thick clots of blood. A chain cut through the air with a whoosh, coming down on his broken ribs.
The short, hard fight ended as abruptly as it had begun. The assailants, having picked up their sticks and chains, quietly got into their cars. A police car drove up to the beaten thimbles. The police never rush to the scene of a crime. The guardians of order wrapped their hands behind their backs and dragged the hapless players to the nearest police station.

***

There was no particular happiness on the faces of the employees and the owner of the video salon. Tied to chairs in the far corner of the room, they sniffed loudly, doused from head to toe with gasoline, and gloomily watched as a visitor with tattooed breasts, peeking out from under a striped tennis shirt, scrupulously poured gasoline on TVs, video equipment, walls... His friend glumly held a new six-shot revolver in his hand, telling his partner what else he thought he should be looking at.
"Don't forget the flowers."
By "flowers," he meant vases of violets, cacti, and a potted palm tree. The canister was empty. The visitors headed for the exit.
"We'll come back tomorrow," the one in the t-shirt said instead of saying goodbye.
"Closer to the evening," - added the one who had a tattoo on his chest.
"If there's no money, we'll throw a match."
***

The elegant brown-haired man brushed the dust off his snow-white shirt. The car was speeding down Victory Avenue.
"Nice work, huh?"
"What's so cool about it? We haven't caught them all yet."
The brown-haired man frowned.
"Khanya, what's next?"
"We go to the central supermarket, then to the Aurora cinema. We need to visit all the places where Ahmed did business."

***

Broken faces, screaming in the crowd, caps scattered on the pavement and crushed - different parts of the city, different times, different people. The same thing happened over and over again.
Cars scrambled out of their seats, speeding away. A few fellows are left lying on the pavement.

Only in one place, there was no fight - near the supermarket on Korneichuk Avenue. A bald-headed man of about thirty-five threw down his thimbles and was the first to rush towards Khanya.
"Vladik, wait! Let me say a few words to Oleg."
The brown-haired man thoughtfully blocked the way. In his fist - brass knuckles.
Khanya got out of the car.
"Let him go."
Pleshyvyi shuffled amusingly, making a semicircle around Vladik.
"Oleg, I agree with everything... Take this." - In his outstretched hand, he held out a stack of money, a gold chain, and a few rings.
– "All the proceeds for today."
Khanya took the money. Counted it. Then he gave some of it back.
"All bald men are lucky. How about you? Not bad for a part-time job..."
A strange, wandering smile. The stare of black eyes. A pause that lasted too long.
"You gave Ahmed half. You'll give me a third. Isn't that a deal that's profitable to everyone? If you want to change anything, you'll lose everything, starting with your health..."
"I understand. I won't let you down!"
"Let's go!"
Vladik hid the brass knuckles in his pants pockets.
"He was smart," he said over his shoulder as they drove away from the department store.
Pleshyvyi was still standing by the curb, watching them.
"He's got good instincts," Khanya said.
"How many times had he seen us before, and only today, he rushed like a dog to our feet as if he knew everything beforehand. Apparently, the prison had taught him a lot."
"He was in prison for a point," agreed the brown-haired man.
"That's enough for today."
A weighty wad of money lay between the seats.

"You'll have dinner at the "Dynamo" restaurant - it's quieter there. And the trash there are all their own."
"Khanya, are you coming with us?"
"No. I have to meet someone in "Kiev" restaurant."
Vova Baranovsky, a heavyweight boxer from Donetsk, was playing with his chain behind him.
"Khanya, should I come with you?"
"You'll have a rest today like everyone else."

***

Pleshyvyi with carefully combed eyebrows and a bushy mustache counted the bills on the table in front of him. His eyes were squinted, and his face showed irritation. With annoyance, he spat under his feet, where empty bottles and cigarette butts lay strewn about.
"You shouldn't have given it to them. We would have..."
Pleshyvyi raised his eyes angrily at the red-haired player:
""Shut up, coward. In the past, you had to show your courage. Nowadays, everyone has become smart, and as soon as something happens, they run in the bushes."
After a pause:
"That's it for today. Let's go. Today is not our day."

***

Vladimir Baranovsky was sitting at a restaurant table, embracing a brown-haired woman in a black, short dress. Baranovsky felt like a royal. Memories of the day's events pleasantly tingled his nerves. The flashes of violence, the sounds of gunfire, and the screams of his rivals still echoed in his ears.
The glow of multicolored lights shimmered merrily overhead, reflecting in the glasses full of whiskey. The musicians played popular songs with a bored look, creating the illusion of an

ordinary evening. The gray-haired vocalist, ignoring the dark figures at the tables, sang intimately about first love.

"It's hot," - languidly moaned the blonde under the weight of Baranovsky holding her tight while dancing. – "Half a life for a breath of fresh air..."

The boxer from Donetsk obediently followed the blonde towards the exit. Vladik, in a wide-open snow-white shirt, perhaps the most sober of the whole company, appreciated her insanely short skirt.

After descending the stairs downstairs, they stepped out onto the plaza in front of the main entrance. The coolness of the evening pleasantly refreshed the faces heated by the dance. Baranovsky's hands slipped under the woman's skirt. Like a hungry, lustful male, Baranovsky kneaded the woman's firm buttocks, becoming more and more aroused.

"Not here. There are people around. We don't need onlookers."

The blonde playfully pulled Baranovsky with her into the darkness, around the corner of the building.

"Shall we smoke?"

The click of a lighter. The smoke of cigarettes. Greedily staring at the hooker's breasts, Baranovsky stealthily walked around the corner of the building. With one hand, he lifted the woman's skirt. With the other, he hastily unbuttoned his pants, trying to free his excited cock.

"What a gorgeous ass you have! Why didn't I know you before?" Whispered Baranowski in the woman's ear. The blonde deftly twisted around and bounced aside with a quiet laugh.

"Because she doesn't sleep with assholes like you." - A short, broad-shouldered figure suddenly emerged from the evening twilight. – "Tell me how you had fun today."

Baranovsky looked down at Manyunya, unable to squeeze out a word. He could only feel his shirt suddenly sticking to his back from cold sweat. Vladik, a dozen friends, familiar cops, ready at any moment to close their eyes or, on the contrary, to intervene -

everything remained behind some boundary, a line. At that moment, there was only one reality - empty, transparent eyes, drilling the brain with contempt and malice, chewed ears, and a short nose. And the woman who, like a spider, had trapped him. Somewhere nearby - he couldn't see it, but he could clearly feel it - gray shadows flickered in the twilight.

"What happened to Ahmed? Where is he? Where is Lali?"

The heavyweight boxer swallowed his saliva with difficulty. Fear made it hard for him to speak. His voice shook.

"I don't know. I swear! Vladik said he wouldn't bother anyone else."

"I see. Your Vladik's turn will come, too. Where's Khanya?"

"He went out by the Kiev restaurant. He's meeting someone."

"You're not lying?"

"I'm not lying. I'm telling the truth. Trust me!"

There was a plea in his voice.

"So what are we going to do with you?" - Manyunya laughed, enjoying the fear on Baranovsky's face. – "Well, rest for now. We'll meet again. And very soon."

***

Vladik immediately sensed that Baranovsky was not well. He came back with a sour face. The brown-haired man had seen such an expression once before, about five years ago, in the prison camp. Then, on New Year's Eve, several prisoners had raped the former supermarket director. After that, he had come into the barracks and sat down on the edge of a stool silently, without raising his eyes.

"Where did you leave the blonde?"

Vladik's hand rested on the boxer's shoulder.

"Chased her away. She's a stupid girl."

"Right, we'll find a better one."

"To say or not to say?" - The thought was whirling in his head. – "It's too late anyway. They're already at the Kiev restaurant. If the others find out that I gave Khanya up... They might not find out. I wish I had been down there, not alone..."

Despite his formidable appearance and the title of master of sports in boxing of international class, Baranovsky, in real life, was not as brave as he seemed. He was bold only in the ring or in a gang behind the backs of others. As a matter of fact, he had once joined boxing to overcome his natural cowardice.

Pouring half a glass of vodka, Baranovsky gulped it down piecemeal, drinking the remnants of Fanta.

***

"There's no one here! Fucker! He lied to us!"

Manyunya listened indifferently, leaning against the hood of the car. A blonde woman was smoking nearby.

Manyunya, a large middle-aged man with straight black hair and tanned skin, stood leaning against the hood of his car. The car was expensive and probably had more power under the hood than most cars on this street. Manyunya was wearing a black t-shirt that emphasized his muscular figure and dark jeans that tightened his short athletic legs.

He listened to the conversations of those around him but didn't participate, as if he was only preoccupied with his own thoughts. His dark eyes were staring into the distance, and there was complete indifference to what was going on around him.

A blonde woman was smoking next to him. Her blond, almost white hair was loose around her shoulders, and the bright red lipstick on her lips made her smile even more noticeable. In her hand was a cigarette, cheap and smelly, which she held with such carelessness as if it were part of her image. The smoke from the cigarette rose slowly upward, filling the air with the thick, cloying odor of tobacco that mingled with her perfume - cheap and sweet, like a candy store.

The woman raised her head from time to time to glance at Manyunya, and her blue eyes sparkled with interest and curiosity. There was something defiant in her gaze as if she had just fucked all those guys in tracksuits and was now enjoying her power over them.

"I think this: Baranovsky was telling the truth. Khanya really came out here. This fox is a sly one." After a long silence, said Manyunya.

"He knows what he's afraid of." Replied in agreement with the boss, one of his subordinates.

"He knows... Let him live a little longer. We will definitely catch him."

***

Khanya was sitting at a table in the restaurant of the Kiev Hotel. He was alone, but he didn't seem lonely. Khanya dined, periodically flipping through the pages of his notebook as if he were looking for something important or trying to remember something he had forgotten. His gaze was fixed on the pages, and he ate almost mechanically, not paying attention to the taste of the food.

The restaurant was full. There were no free tables. A familiar waiter, recognizing Khanya, hooked him up with a noisy group of people who were celebrating someone's birthday. It was a fairly large group of people of various ages, having fun and joking with each other. It was obvious that they worked at the same company. By the time Khanya arrived, the guests were already quite drunk and in good spirits. Their laughter and conversations filled the entire hall. None of them paid attention to the strange guy at the far end of the table.

The moment the men from Ahmed's gang entered the restaurant, the company rose from their seats to listen to a long toast in honor of the jubilee, unwittingly creating a living wall between predators and their prey. Khanya was the only one who remained seated. He was preoccupied with his own thoughts. All this merriment did not concern him.

When the company sat down again, the unwanted guests were already descending the stairs toward the exit. Khanya was saved by fortune. He had been very lucky that day.

CHAPTER IV

Violetta sat on the bed in her small but cozy room. Her brown eyes were fixed on the window, behind which pale pink clouds were scattering under the sunset rays. The girl wrapped her arms around her knees as if trying to hold in all the pain and fear she felt. Her heart was beating faster than usual, thoughts swirling in her head, giving her no rest.

Violetta waited for the phone call. It could give her joy and relief, or it could increase her fears and calmness. She waited for the call from Oleg, the guy who had suddenly become her whole world.

"Oleg, please don't leave me like this - like an unwanted toy that has been played with and forgotten the morning after... I have never been so good as with you. Why don't you say anything? I'll give you anything you want... Oleg!" - she whispered desperately, looking at her phone.

But the phone was silent. It was cold and indifferent.

"It's hard without you..." - whispered the girl into the void again.

Violetta felt lost and alone. Fear and uncertainty overwhelmed her. Was she really just a toy to him, forgotten the day after the game? Or maybe he had already found another or gone back to one of his former lovers? The thought of that burned her from the inside out.

But what Violetta feared most of all was that she would lose him forever, that she would never hear his voice again, never see his smile, never feel his embrace.

Doubt. Fear. Uncertainty.

Violetta felt sinking deeper into despair with each passing minute and into the stillness that was destroying her. The girl tried to fight her feelings, but she felt her strength leaving her.

Was it really so painful to love?

A calm, quiet child, as Violetta was considered by her parents, suddenly went out of obedience, turning into a fervent, passionate woman, ready to do anything in the name of a few moments of happiness. Neither the girl herself nor her parents knew how to behave. Like most mothers and fathers, they realized that such a situation would happen sooner or later, but when it did, the parents were completely helpless in front of their own children. Is Violetta someone's mistress? Is Violetta in bed with a man? Such a thought simply did not fit in their minds!

Violetta's parents were confused. They knew that first love could be both beautiful and destructive, and they feared the consequences for Violetta. At the same time, the parents realized that their daughter had to make her own decisions. Only she and no one else.

Neither mother nor father knew how to behave. They wanted to support their daughter, but they did not know how to do it. They had never talked to their daughter about love, let alone intimacy. And was it ever possible to talk about such things with a child?

A tense silence hung in the apartment. The family members hardly spoke to each other. Violetta's older brother, a phlegmatic fat man, chuckled quietly as he watched his parents' shocked state and his sister's apathetic mood. He was the only one amused by it all.

"He won't call or come. I've been abandoned." Leaden pincers of longing squeezed her shoulders. With a familiar movement, Violetta tossed back her brown hair. Leaning against the window sill, she looked out the open window. A wave of despair and pain poured over her, pulling her down into the abyss of misery.

***

The atmosphere of Gosha's apartment was instantly convincing: it was the home of a bachelor who rarely was at home. It was a place that clearly did not know a woman's hand and where functionality was prioritized over aesthetics.

The shabby wallpaper barely covered the carpet from Gosha's grandmother's youth, creating an atmosphere of decay and abandonment. A pennant with Lenin's profile and the inscription "The Best Workplace" hung crookedly over the low sofa with broken legs. There were few books in the bookcase, but it was full of all kinds of often unnecessary trifles, such as crooked nails, cigarette butts, a dirty bra forgotten by someone, Marx's "Capital" and other junk. The pictures on the walls told about Gosha's childhood, and a newspaper clipping about the search for criminals, beginning with the words "Wanted..." and neatly pinned with pins to the wallpaper, laconically told about the apartment owner's youth.

Khanya, half-listening to Gosha's monologue, occasionally interrupted by Korotyshka's phrases, looked regretfully at the new VCR. The beer bottles on the lid and a few muddy stains clearly did not adorn the creation of the Japanese company "Sony."

Life in such an apartment could seem depressing and devoid of joy. But for Gosha, it was his personal space, a place where he could relax and be himself.

The doorbell rang sharply and unexpectedly.

"Who is it?"

Korotyshka hissed, which meant he was worried. Gosha catlike darted into the hallway. Khanya, as if by accident, leaned against the doorjamb.

"Who's there?" - Gosha asked, throwing a double chain on the door.
"I'm looking for Gosha," came from behind the door.
"Just a minute. I'll call him."
Gosha ducked under the sofa and soon returned to the door with a grenade in his hand. The lock clicked. A curly-haired man in a denim jacket was shuffling from foot to foot in the stairwell.
"Gosha, thank God you're home."
"Alone?"
"Alone, what?"
"Are you alone?"
"Me? Yes, of course. What, I don't understand?"
Gosha threw off the chain. Curly fell into the hallway.
"Only you and Khanya can save us."
"Hmm. Who'd have thought it."
"We're here..." - Curly faltered at the sight of the grenade.
"It's for uninvited guests," - Gosha reassured. Small eyes smiled paternally from under wheaten eyebrows.
"Tell me," smiled the owner in a friendly manner, carelessly dropping the grenade into the shoebox.
The grenade hit the bottom with a thud. Curly wrinkled his nose.
"You know - we tried to live without disturbing anyone," Curly began, unbuttoning his jean jacket. - "Quietly making money..."
"Good money?" - Gosha put in.
"Well... it depends," - Curly hesitated.
"You can't earn good money quietly," - the owner concluded thoughtfully.
"Gosha, this is a serious matter. Two scumbags came to us, to the video salon, put us under the barrels, and poured gasoline on us. They promised to burn us."
"So they'll burn him if they promised."
Curly was sweating.
"We have to do something. We can't just run to the garbage men."

"That's right. The police won't help here. Those morons rarely help anyone except for a bribe. They're thinking about their stomachs, not your safety. But you must understand us, too. Your money's yours, but what's the point of us getting shot?"
"Gosha, I know how to be grateful!"
"I hope you realize that money as such is unlikely to interest our friends."
"Fall into a share - and a part of the profit is yours."
Gosha sighed tiredly:
"Okay, let's drive up. We'll figure out who blocked your oxygen, and now go away. I can't invite you to the room: the girls are in bed. They're probably waiting for me."
"Do you like to fuck two at the same time?" - Curly grinned sourly.
"Or three. My health allows it so far."
The palms of their hands clasped together in a muffled handshake.
"Let's go!"
"I'm waiting."
The door slammed. Satisfied, Gosha returned to the room.
"Everything is clear. The boys gave them a big scare. Now, we will protect them from us."
Korotyshka's face expressed complete satisfaction with the world's vanity.
"Did he know your address before?" - Khanya asked calmly.
"No..." - Gosha froze in the doorway in surprise. - "How?"
Korotyshka snorted loudly. Khanya changed the tape in the tape recorder. A hoarse voice. Spanish tunes. Strange music. I wonder where that cassette came from in Gosha's den.
"Not much good. If he found it, sooner or later, others will find you too."

***

Among the countless ways in which some people control others, two are the most effective: health threats and promises of material benefits. In other words, in order to force an abstract person to do something (or not to do something), it is necessary to offer, preferably in an accessible and understandable form, a certain amount of money or a number of services promising benefits. As practice shows, most people are ready to sell anything and everything for material benefits. The main thing is to give them some moral justification for their actions. However, there are cases when this technique either does not work or people are simply unwilling to spend money. Then, a person is put before a choice: either agree and live or go to a nearby cemetery. A reliable, centuries-proven method. And then it all depends on how serious the issue is and what kind of people are dealing with it. As a rule, the corpses appear in two cases: when the case involved stupid morons persistently looking for a way to prison, or professionals, cold-bloodedly weighing all pros and cons.

Khanya's opponents were characterized by a pathological arrogance born of chronic impunity, but all of them were cowardly when their tails were tucked. In particular, Manyunya had never been a brave man. However, due to his own limitations and thought retardation, the sense of fear came to him much later than to a normal person. Most often, it manifested itself after the conflict was over. Nevertheless, the case of Ahmed shocked the wrestler. The disappearance of the owner was unambiguously associated with the name of Oleg Khanin, known among the criminals as Khanya. No one assumed that Akhmed or Khanya was capable of going to the extreme and, after it, so openly brazenly attacked the opponent. The bulk of Ahmed's "associates" scattered at once while the rest waited. Hassan and a few of Ahmed's loyal friends remained with Manyunya.

Khanya scrupulously made sure that his rivals were deprived of sources of profit. Thimbles, for example, were still played, but Khanya, not Ahmed, took the spit. The cooperatives, which had a stable income, one after another, were taken over by Khanya. This was often done in the following way. Several criminals came to the chairman of the cooperative and told him to pay the amount which he could not afford. Otherwise, they promised to stab him to death. After the uninvited guests left, a "good acquaintance," who happened to be nearby "quite by chance," approached the owner of the establishment and recommended that he turn to Khanya. Oleg, of course, did not refuse and came to the rescue absolutely free, so to speak, out of kindness. Then "a good friend" appeared again and threw into the heads of cooperators the following idea: "The guys came to help only because they treat you well, but every time, no one is going to risk their heads only out of altruism. That's why it makes sense to offer the guys a share and sleep well. Here, a more real sum of money was called. There was only one thing left - to agree. Moreover, like Curly, they themselves came to Khanya, asking him to take over their patronage.

From time to time, there were problems with those who doubted whether they needed such patronage and security. In this case, the situation was repeated with more serious consequences. There was no choice. The business prospered.

There were various methods of taking profits, from the most sophisticated (when money passed through a tangled maze of hands and papers so that many people did not realize who they were paying) to the simple and crude, as Khanya had resorted to after Ahmed's disappearance.

Far from limiting himself to cutting off sources of income, Khanya actually showed that there were no limits to him. No limits whatsoever. He behaved uncompromisingly and brutally. Demonstrably tough. Khanya's brutality sometimes bordered on cruelty and sadism.

In the crime world, every day, someone is threatened with being killed, cut into pieces, or taken out into the woods. It is part of the "good tone." However, threats are rarely put into practice. As a rule, compromise solutions are always found.

Khanya didn't threaten. He did what he thought was useful and necessary for him. The opinions of others existed solely to improve his own conclusions, but in no way could they change the course of his thoughts. Knowing this, both Manyunya and Hassan had no doubt that Khanya would stop at nothing until he knocked their team out of Kiev.

For Manyunya, who had taken Ahmed's place, there was no other way but to leave Kiev. At the same time, everyone realized two things. First, Manyunya could only earn money the way he did with Akhmed. Second, only in Kiev could Manyunya earn as much as he had so far. Therefore, no one doubted that Akhmed's men would try to return to Kiev at the first opportunity.

***

Morning. Phone call.

"Khanya, hello!"

The elegant brown-haired man's voice sounded muffled. It was either the distance (he usually called from the other side of the city) or the alcohol he had drunk the previous night.

"Do we have time today?"

Vladik always asked like that when he wasn't going to do business.

"Do you have anything to offer?"

"It would be good to hit the punching bags in the gym and relax in the sauna with girls after the training."

"Okay, call the gym back. Have them make sure no strangers are there."

"Of course."

Long beeps on the phone.

***

Sitting on a bench at the entrance to the boxing gym, Baranovsky was visibly nervous, keeping his eyes on the street. Khanya appeared at a quarter to three, driving up to the sports center in a black Volga. Next to him was an unshaven Korotyshka. Behind him loomed the figures of Gosha in his unchanged gray knit sweater and Vladik. Vova rose sharply to meet them.

"Manyunya said that you're finished," the boxer said to the brunet instead of greeting him. – "And everyone with you."

The blood rushed to Khanya's face and immediately rushed back. "Where did you see him?"

"This morning, outside the Rus Hotel. Manyunya and Hasan aren't leaving forever. They'll all be back soon."

Khanya smirked, looking at Baranovsky.

"If you think you said something original and witty, you're wrong."

"He said..."

"I have been promised to be stabbed since I was thirteen years old. As long as I live. What are you afraid of? You're so strong. Master of Sports in boxing. International class."

There was a flicker of contempt in his smile. Khanya put his bag from one shoulder to the other, and, walking past the boxer, he headed for the entrance to the sports center.

"Are you going to train?" - Vladik asked Baranovsky.

"I want to rest. I'm sick of the gym. All my life in boxing."

"Of course. You're a professional. We're amateurs. I'm gonna go work out for my health."

Vladik was the first to give a handshake. Baranovsky sluggishly said goodbye:

"I'm not needed, aren't I?"

"It's our day off."

***

Khanya was practicing a jumping knee strike. After each new blow, the boxing bag jingled, swaying from side to side like a drunken boxer.

Khanya stopped, took a breath, and brushed the sweat off his forehead. In this gym, amidst the iron and sweat, he could forget everything that happened outside the gym. Here, with every punch and every jump, he was leaving his worries and stresses behind.

The anxiety he carried in his heart, born of days gone by, was becoming less and less acute. It was receding, retreating into the depths of his subconscious like a beast that had been cornered. With each stroke Khanya gave, the anxiety lessened, but it didn't go away completely.

Khanya's driver looked into the gym.

"I thought you were in the sauna."

"Hi, Rakhit, I have a business to attend to," Korotyshka slid off the bench.

"Later. Khanya, I met Baranovsky on the street. He looked a little depressed."

"It's his age," Vladik said, dropping the weights to the floor. – "The consequences of blows missed during the period of puberty."

A series of carefully practiced punches threw the punching bag against the wall. Khanya stared at the target swinging creakily on the rusty chain and felt the desire to train to leave him. It was replaced by an unconscious sense of fear, an animal fear that lives in all of us and is waiting to be found.

The events of the past weeks flashed before his eyes again (for the umpteenth time!), flashing bright colors and fading into the twilight of his brain. Behind the outwardly calm, somewhat phlegmatic appearance, there were nerves taut as strings, ready to break at any moment from a careless touch.

What does fear mean? Where are its roots, in the name of which it wakes us up in cold sweat in the middle of the night? Even when you are perfectly safe, the realization that someone wishes you harm inexorably impacts your thoughts. It may be invisible, inaudible, or imperceptible, but it is an impact.

"What's on your mind? Let's go to the sauna." - Vladik's voice sounded carefree.

Elegant brown hair. A fan of snow-white shirts and white clothes in general. Immaculately dressed. Two prior convictions, both for his own stupidity. Because of an excessive fondness for women and drugs. Moderately stingy. Egotistical. They'd always gotten along fine, even though Khanya hated that type of people, which, of course, no one could guess.

***

The water was pleasantly caressing his body, flowing down his legs to the wooden grate. A wave of tension washed away with it. Khanya stood under the shower. He opened the blue faucet to full power and put his face under the scalding jets of cold water.

Vladik was frolicking in the sauna. He liked to have sex with the hookers on the top shelf of the sauna, despite the heat. Languorous moans mixed with profanity and laughter came to the shower from behind the closed door. Korotyshka and Gosha were swimming in the pool. Rakhit was munching cookies in the recreation room with his sheet-wrapped legs thrown over the back of a chair. He was only marginally interested in girls. They were not interested in him at all.

Footsteps behind him. Someone approached quietly from behind, gently touching his shoulder. Khanya slowly opened his eyes. Lowered his head and looked around. Her loose black hair fell in waves over her firm, naked breasts. Almond-shaped eyes. The rounded features of an immaculate female body.

"What do you want, Rina?"

Her full name was Marina. The woman's hand parted the cold jets of water above her head.

"You'll freeze, you'll get sick, you'll die... What will we do without you?"

Her voice was the epitome of resignation, like the rustling of grass. "You'll live like before, like others."

"What does it mean "like others"? There's no such thing as "others." Everyone lives his own life, and everyone is a part of the life of someone else. These are your words, Oleg."

"You have a good memory."

"Only memory?"

The tips of her long nails gently touched the muscles of his chest, slid to his shoulder blades, and then the girl moved down. Khanya felt the touch of hot lips, a wave of heat and desire, a wave of pleasure piercing every cell in his body. After a moment's hesitation, Oleg leaned forward, lifted the girl kneeling in front of him, and kissed her on the lips ...

"I'm sorry, Rina. I'm tired today."

For a thousandth, no, a hundredth of a thousandth of a second, lightning flashed and dissolved into the pupils of almond-shaped eyes.

"I know. You've had some hard days."

The girl walked out of the shower with a proud, leisurely gait, wiping her wet hair with a towel. She was leaving, but she was encouraging me to follow her. The man stared after her, watching the drops of water dripping down her naked body, unable to take his eyes off her shapely legs.

Khanya felt anger, a beastly anger at himself. There had been a time when he had wanted to live with Marina, but things had never worked out - not enough time, not enough conditions, not enough God knows what else. Something always interfered. And now Marina herself came, and he pushed her away. After all, it was because of him that she had joined all of them in that damned sauna today.

Vladik's laughter and floundering in the pool caused irritation, annoyance, and a feeling of irrevocably wasted time.

His eyelids drooped. "What's happening to me?" - Khanya thought.

Scraps of thoughts, images, and meaningless words flashed through his mind.

A feeling of dissatisfaction. A longing.

Brown hair. Brown eyes. A proud gait. Violetta.

CHAPTER V

"Letta, I want to see you."

"I don't want to see you."

Pause.

"I feel bad. You know."

"Me too."

"Then why, why don't you want to see me?"

"You'll leave me. Better sooner than later. No one will love you the way I do, but I don't want to be a toy. That's what I've decided."

"It's nonsense, total nonsense, everything you say."

Silence. Frustration. Irritation.

"Oleg."

"Yes."

"Tell me something. Please."

"I don't want to talk on the phone. I want to talk to you and see your eyes."

"There's no other way."

"Letta, I'm standing outside your house, and I'm waiting for you."

"Don't wait. I won't come out."

"Then I'll come to you myself."

"No, thank you. I have parents and a brother."
"I don't care about that. If you don't come out, I'll break down the door and come in."
He heard laughter in response. Khanya hung up irritably. He left the phone box. He crossed to the opposite side of the street and sat cross-legged at the edge of the road in the middle of the sidewalk. At that moment, he didn't care what passers-by thought of him.

***

"I've been waiting for you for so long..."
The girl's slender fingers ran through the black strands of her lover's hair.
"Time flew by so quickly. It was like we never parted."
"It wasn't."
Violetta laid her head back on the pillow.
"It had been a long time ago, a long time ago. Time stretched on forever..."
The mirror reflected her luxurious hair scattered on the bed. Sensual lips. Eyes wide open.
Khanya looked at the beautiful girl with admiration.
"You're just like a baby... Or a kitten."
"A kitten or a baby?"
"Both."
Hot breathing flowed into a muffled, sweet moan.
"Oleg, are you not embarrassed to lie with me on the bed in front of a half-wall mirror? No? And I'm embarrassed. Anyway, you don't love me."
"There's something more than love."
"What is it?"
"Caprice."
"Caprice?"

"Yes. "The only difference between eternal love and caprice is that caprice lasts a little longer," I think it was great Oscar Wilde who said that."
"How prosaic."
"But fair enough. You are my caprice, and I am yours."
"I don't want to be a caprice. I don't even want to be your caprice. I'm not a doll."
"Do I treat you like a doll?"
"No, but still. Don't you believe in love?"
"Love. I don't deny it. After all, without love, as well as without faith, life is meaningless and empty."
In the next room, Rakhit was dozing on the rug. This guy had a dog's sense of direction, for which he was valued no less than for his ability to drive cars.
After the sauna, Khanya disappeared. He disappeared very abruptly and unexpectedly. Vladik and Korotyshka were drunk and in the company of hookers.
They had not paid attention to Khanya's disappearance. Marina also discreetly dressed and left. Only Gosha was disturbed by Khanya's behavior.
"Listen, Rakhit, you need to get in the car and go get Oleg."
"Go where?"
"Go anywhere, but you have to find the boss.
"Find him where? He didn't say where he was going."
Small eyes from under wheaten eyebrows looked down unkindly at the thin figure.
"Khanya is like a son to me. If anything happens to him, you'll be the first to go after Ahmed. You know it."
Rakhit swore but got into the car. Where to go? Where to look? He made a few loops around Kiev. His intuition told him to go to Lesnoy district. And sure enough. He drove up at the moment when a slender girl in a long skirt with a slit approached the guy sitting on the pavement. Khanya was not surprised to see Rakhit.

Khanya and the girl silently got into the car in the back seat. The girl lay on Khanya's lap, setting her lips up for a kiss.

While Khanya was in the bedroom, Rakhit had thoroughly examined the refrigerator (despite his morbidly skinny appearance, Rakhit liked eating delicious food), watched a movie on TV, and was now dozing on the carpet. However, he did not want to sleep, and he involuntarily listened to the scraps of words coming from the bedroom.

"Without love, as without faith, life is empty..."

Rakhit wondered. What was Khanya talking about? Curious, what drives this man's actions? People much older than him obey him without complaint. Moreover, among them, there are many recidivists with a long record.

Rakhit remembered a year-old discussion.

A smoky room. Three voices in a cloud of tobacco smoke.

The first one was soft and tired:

"What is it to kill a man? You take out a shiv, stab it under the heart, and an inhabitant of planet Earth sleeps easy."

The second voice, exhaling a breath of booze, was rough and hard, "Indeed. You take out the barrel and pull the trigger... A piece of cake!"

"It's no use dying like that," Khanya's voice cut into the discourse.

"Why not?"

"Before killing, you should show a man blue skies, pink castles ... So that he leaves life with a pale pink feeling at the moment when he wants to live the most."

The thick carpet warmed his back pleasantly. Out of boredom, Rakhit started looking at the bookshelves. Thousands of books. Had Khanya read them all? Who was Khanya?

***

Marina looked at her sleeping son. The three-year-old was sleeping, smiling in his sleep. His chubby little hands were hugging a toy green elephant.

Despite its modesty and some old things, Marina's apartment looks cozy and warm. The first thing that catches the eye is the perfect cleanliness. Not a speck of dust on the windowsills, no scattered things. Everything is neatly stored, each thing in its place. This is not just a dwelling. It is a reflection of her resilience and determination despite all the difficulties of life.

Neatly folded things are placed on a very old bed, which stands opposite the window. A bulky, massive closet is set in the corner of the room, towering majestically over all other pieces of furniture. The closet looks somewhat old-fashioned and redundant for such a small room, but it plays an important role. It holds all of her belongings, from clothes and bedding to books.

There is a cheap rug on the floor, worn and scuffed from endless use. It may not look particularly attractive, but it adds a bit of coziness to this humble room and serves as protection from the cold floor during the winter months.

There are faded blue curtains hanging from the windows, which glow dimly in the sunlight. They were probably bright and beautiful once, but the time and the sun have done their work. The woman hesitated for a while, then stood up abruptly, taking her keys and a few coins... The public phone was not far from the house.

The child was asleep. His mother soon returned. She threw off her robe from her shoulders, which cast a matte whiteness, and took her time to change her clothes. Carefully, so as not to wake her son, she kissed his forehead. She left the house, quietly closing the door behind her.

***

The police station. Opposite the sergeant, a fifth-year medical student was sobbing. The policeman sighed mundanely. How fed up was he with it all! What is all the fuss about if someone was robbed? Such things happen several times a day, and she was robbed for the first time in her life. She says they took 1,000 or 2,000 worth of stuff. The policeman wondered how an ordinary student could have so much money.

"Calm down, Miss. We'll get to the bottom of this. Everything is in order."

"I came out of the subway, "Khreshchatyk." A woman came up to me."

"What did she look like? How was she dressed?"

"How? She was so spectacular. Black curly hair. Eyes a little oblong, I think. Jewelry was all over her."

"What do you mean all over?"

"Well, you know. Earrings, cross-chain, wrist bracelet, rings."

"Further."

"She says: "Miss, I'm sorry, I've arranged to meet my lover, but my husband is following me. If you don't mind, tell my boyfriend - there he stands, near the phone booth, that I can't go to him now, but tomorrow, in the morning, I'll call him in the office ". I walked there and handed over everything she asked for. The man said "Thank you" and …

"Pulled out a gas can and shot you in the face."

"Yes, he did. God, I almost passed out. He tore off my wedding ring, earrings, and necklace, took my purse with money and makeup, took off my shoes..."

The woman sobbed.

"You didn't try to scream? It's a public place."

"I didn't have time. It all happened so fast!"

"What did the man look like?"

"He was unkempt, with stubble. He smelled of alcohol, too. You'll find them, won't you?"

There's hope in her voice, pleading. The sergeant slammed the folder shut with a confident gesture.

"We'll definitely find them."

And he thought to himself, "No one will search for them."

***

Two shadows under the chestnut leaves.

"Shall we go together?"

"The son is alone in the apartment. You go by yourself. Don't haggle. Whatever Grandma Valya gives you, that's what you'll get."

Grandma Valya, Valyuha, the bony bitch... When she was young, she had a prettier name: Suzanna. An unusual name for a woman born in the 1940s after the Second World War. She was said to be one of Moscow's most famous hookers. Her beauty was ravishing and striking. Long golden hair that glistened in the sun, firm skin that glowed with youth, and deep emerald eyes that spoke a thousand unspoken words. Her caresses cost a lot of money, but people like Fima Odessky and Yashka Kosoy never skimped. After Marat Mecheny stabbed his accomplice because of her and slit his wrists in a pre-trial detention cell in December 1963, the rumor about the lovely girl swirled through countless prisons and camps in the Soviet country.

But... It's all in the past. Time has mercilessly warped Suzanna's once beautiful appearance. Time is an inexorable artist who repaints human lives in darker shades. Time does not choose its victims. It simply does its work. And like any artist, time leaves its marks on its work.

Suzanna grew old. Her skin became flabby and soaked, like an old sack that had been left out in the rain. Each of her former lovers had left behind dirty traces on her body and on her soul. Each of them leaving her had taken some of her beauty with them. Her golden hair turned gray and dull like a winter landscape. Her eyes lost their luster, leaving only a cold reflection of a hard life.

Her gentle name, Suzanna, was a thing of the past. Now, she was just an old woman. She made a living by reselling stolen goods, and it made people squeamish and disgusted. She lived in a dirty apartment that smelled like a homeless dog kennel. She was alone, with no family no children.

But even in this state, even in this ugly shell, somewhere deep inside her, there was still Suzanna. Time can change the appearance, but it cannot change the soul. Inside this old woman still lived the same woman who was once the queen of the criminal underworld.

Time had changed her body, but it hadn't touched the part of the woman that remained unchanged despite everything that went on around her in her life.

Valya was old and ugly, but she was still the woman who had once been a queen. And that was something no one could take away from her.

The attitude toward Valya, with a dash of sympathy and pity, was fairly even in all strata of the criminal world. Only one man with a soft and tired voice laughed and said, "Naive idiots! You think you're dealing with a poor woman? She could buy all of you if she wanted to! She doesn't want your stolen things. She buys and resells this shit just to relieve her loneliness."

***

Marina went to her friend's house. Gave her a bracelet, rings, chain with a cross... She returned home. The son was still asleep, not noticing the absence of his mother.

After midnight, the doorbell rang. An unshaven man, without taking off his dirty shoes, went into the kitchen and carelessly threw the money on the kitchen table.

"There's around five hundred in here. Your money."
"Get your hands off me!" - The girl recoiled squeamishly from the greasy palm that unceremoniously touched her thighs. Her voice, normally soft and pleasant, became a sharp hissing arrow piercing the silence of the room.

The man, more mountain-like than human, grinned, revealing a row of uneven yellow teeth. He was confident in his power, confident that money could buy anything he wanted.

"Rina, with your looks, you could make a lot more money overnight," - he said in a tone as if he were offering her a ticket to a cruise on a luxury yacht on the Atlantic Ocean.

"None of your business," - she cut him off, her voice determined and confident. Marina had never sold herself for money, even in her most difficult moments. Her answer sounded like a stone thrown through a glass window - clear and concise, leaving little room for further discussion.

He shrugged, pulling a wad of money out of his pocket.

"Well, well... relax. I can help, after all," - he continued as if offering her a way out of a desperate situation.

- There's three thousand. Maybe more. I haven't counted. For a few hours in your bed with you."

"Fuck you. Go away!"

The door rattled on the stairwell, silenced footsteps. Marina tiredly sank down next to the crib of her son. Hopelessness squeezed the temples. Burying her face in the pillow, she sobbed.

***

Rakhit was asleep on the carpet with his legs stretched out unnaturally.

"Oleg, there's no one to take me home."

Khanya came up behind her, gently kissing her brown hair.

"You'll have to stay."

"No way! They might kick me out of the house. Let's wake him up."
"Let him sleep. I'll drive you."
Leaning over the sleeping man, the brunet carefully checked the contents of his pants. In a minute, Khanya had the car keys from Rakhit's side pocket.
"Shall we go?"
"You searched him so professionally!"
Khanya's gaze burned ice cold. Letta clung to Khanya's chest.
"I'm sorry, my darling. I didn't mean to hurt you. I just said it by mistake... I'm sorry."

***

In contrast to Rakhit, Khanya drove carefully around the city, not forgetting the rules of the road. "You don't have to respect the laws, but it's good to remember them," Khanya told his friends many times.
"Oleg, does Rakhit work with you?" - Inquisitive gaze of brown eyes.
"Yes, in the same company. At work, he is my driver. After work, he helps me as a friend."
"You must be exploiting him mercilessly."
"What makes you think that?"
"Just a hunch. Does he make good money?"
"Not bad. You sound like a prosecutor."
"I'm interested."
"It's not good for women to be interested in money."
"Why?"
"It has a negative effect on their behavior and their looks, too. Wrinkles, for example."
"Not all men can provide for women. Your views are a little outdated. In today's society, men and women have changed places."

"A man must always remain a man, and a woman must always remain a woman. Otherwise, the balance in nature will be disturbed, and mankind will degenerate."
"By the way, there have been lesbians and gays at all times."
"Homosexual relationships are against the will of the Most High who created us exactly as we are. And what's the use of men when there are so many charming women around?!"
The car stopped on Zhukov Street. A long kiss. The rustle of clothes. The bright, blinding light of the headlights of a random truck.
"When shall we meet again?"
"When you're free, call me. Okay?"
Hot lips. Strong hands. Leaves whispering in the wind. The girl walks quickly towards the house, almost running. She is happy because she is loved. Family, children, position in society, material prosperity - she will have everything she once dreamed of. In her dreams of the future, there is no room for doubts or fears. Violetta believes in her lucky star and is sure that all her dreams will come true. She believes that all this will happen because she can't imagine her future life any other way.

***

"You should have slept."
Khanya entered the room, and without stopping, he threw off his sneakers. Rakhit was leafing through a West German catalog for flower growers.
"Gosha called. There's trouble with Korotyshka. Almost got picked up by the cops."
"How long ago did he call?"
"About ten minutes ago. They went to drink cognac after the sauna. Korotyshka was eager to fight with the cops. The guys had a hard time stopping him. The bad thing is he gets too talkative when he drinks too much. He was telling girls about our business."

"Why didn't Vladik and Gosha stop him?"
"They were drunk. Don't you know Vladik? Or Gosha?"
"Vladik went to jail for a glass of vodka once. Gosha is more careful."
"Gosha?" - You could hear the distaste in Rakhit's voice. – "A bottle of cognac and a glass of beer is the daily norm."
"Where's Korotyshka?"
"They took him to the police station first. Now he's at home. Sleeping."
"Pick him up in the morning. Meet me at Gorky at eleven."
Khanya went into the bathroom. Stuck his head under the faucet. The excessive talkativeness of anyone could hardly help the common cause. "The problems with Korotyshka are the last thing I need," Oleg thought angrily, wiping his face with a terry towel.

***

Korotyshka was characterized by a rare sluggishness and diligence. As a matter of fact, he could not think and did not want to think. The process of thinking caused him a feeling of grief and a hard-to-endure longing. Moderately cowardly, insolent, and swaggering - a typical representative of the young generation of speculators born in the first half of the seventies. In his childhood, he was warmed by the air of Brezhnev's stagnation. In the period of maturation, he, along with everyone else, felt the firm hand of Andropov and the senile marasmus of Chernenko. But the guy really blossomed in the era of Gorbachev's glasnost and democracy.
Korotyshka was picked up by Gosha when the young talent was running up and down Khreshchatyk with a pile of Czech bras. Gosha was just looking for a suitable candidate for the role of "hound." Korotyshka was so eagerly offering goods to familiar and unfamiliar hookers and pimps that Gosha simply could not fail to appreciate the creative possibilities of the future pupil.

A couple of days later, Korotyshka, washed, smoothly shaved, stood in a neat suit at the door of Vnesheconombank, pretending to be a rising star of Soviet chess, who not so long ago returned from the U.S. with a wad of dollars. Cutting into the queue, or rather - into the crowd of those wishing to exchange Soviet rubles for foreign currency, Korotyshka, in an angelic voice (but so that everyone could hear), asked where it was possible to exchange currency for rubles. Two or three people who were sick to death of waiting in vain for their turn would jump out of the crowd. In different interpretations, they would repeat roughly the same thing: "Why do you need to give the currency to the bank? We'll buy it from you at a mutually beneficial rate." Korotyshka took the client aside, hesitated for a moment, then began to bargain. Having reached an agreement, they went their separate ways. That was the end of the first stage.

The second stage was a preliminary meeting, at which Korotyshka introduced the client to Gosha, who played the role of "daddy." "Loving son" could not sell a thousand dollars without the blessing of "daddy." "Daddy" - in glasses and a solid suit - inspired confidence.

The third stage consisted directly of the purchase and sale itself. The client came to the agreed place with the money and, together with "daddy," went home to the seller. At the entrance, Gosha asked to wait. After a while, he would return with the words: "You know, I have unexpected guests, and I wouldn't want them to know that I sell currency. You see, my apartment is small, and I have no privacy. Let's settle up right here in the entryway. I have the dollars with me. At the sight of currency, the buyer was no longer frightened by the dark entryway. Like a donkey after a carrot, he obediently followed the seller. First, the buyer checked whether the dollars were real dollars, then counted them and returned them to the seller. The seller counted the money. The simple procedure ended with the seller taking the money and the buyer being ceremoniously handed a "doll" made up of counterfeit money mixed with one-dollar bills instead of a wad of dollars. At the moment of handing over the "doll," "random passers-by" would appear (at an established signal), diverting attention to themselves. The seller would leave through the passing yard, jump in his car, and disappear. The buyer would walk around for five days in an insane state, then calm down, forget... Korotyshka would reappear at the bank door.

Sometimes, there were mishaps - the buyer brought the same swindlers as the sellers (exchange of "dolls" - and everyone is happy), or ordinary robbers (a friendly meeting with old acquaintances or fights with stabbing).

Khanya carefully observed the actions of "hounds" (like Korotyshka), "throwers" (Gosha and others), "diverters" ("random passers-by"), and drivers who took away the "thieves." There were no problems with the authorities. Where should the victim go? To the police? According to the existing legislation, the victim faced more time for illegal currency transactions than the imaginary seller for fraud. Besides, police officers, prosecutors, and KGB officers often acted as passers-by. Everyone needs money.

Korotyshka grew older and stronger financially from the scams. However, he did not become smarter. As practice shows, most often, money does not shorten but loosens tongues.

***

The old streets of Kiev are characterized by tangled labyrinths of passable houses, yards of all kinds of shapes with countless entrances, exits, and dead ends... Gorky Street was no exception.

Gosha was smoking, sitting on a bench next to Khanya. Korotyshka fell out of a BMW with tinted windows, sniffing and breathing booze. Rakhit stayed behind the wheel.

"I hear your tongue is longer than normal. I'll have it checked. Open your mouth."

Korotyshka blinked his sleepy eyes in confusion.
Khanya stared intently into Korotyshka's eyes.
"Open your mouth, sweetheart. We'll just see what's wrong," - Gosha nodded lullingly.
Korotyshka hesitantly opened his mouth.
Khanya sighed sadly and stood up from the bench.
With a sharp, well-placed fist strike, he swept the fellow off his feet. The back of Korotyshka's head hit the pavement with a thud. His mouth filled with blood. In clots of crimson-black foam floated shards of teeth. Khanya leaned over Korotyshka. Pressed his head against the asphalt. Suddenly, Khanya felt a very strong, uncontrollable sexual excitement, similar to what he felt in bed during lovemaking with Violetta.
"Oleg..." - Korotyshka whispered pitifully, trying to cover his face with his palms.
Several well-placed strokes came down on his half-open lips. A puddle of blood dripped from the back of his head. His eyes began to blur. Everything was floating somewhere, and from far away, a familiar voice addressed to Gosha:
"Take this scum to the doctor. He's saved enough money to have gold teeth put in instead of natural teeth."
The pale faces of tightly bunched guys. The BMWs pull out of the yard. Next to the driver was Khanya. Rakhit looked back. Anxiety in his voice:
"Will he wake up?"
"He'll live."
Khanya turned on the music, closed his eyes, and leaned back in his chair... After everything that had happened, Oleg could not make sense of himself. It seemed that he did what he had to do for the sake of order and justice. Then there is this unpleasant feeling as if he was beaten, not he did it? The feeling of dirt clinging to his body was still there. With an effort of will, Khanya relaxed his

eyes and hands and tried to mentally dissolve into the melody of the song that filled the interior of the car.
Rakhit drove up to the Kiev restaurant. The clock showed a little bit after midday. It was early for lunch, but Khanya was used to early breakfast and early lunch.
"Oleg, are we going out?"
The brunet answered nothing. He was asleep.

CHAPTER VI

The gray-haired professor stood in front of the blackboard, mundanely reading a lecture about Pavlov's scientific activity. His voice sounded monotonous and unemotional as if he were not a human being but a machine recording information into the brains of students.
"Pavlov's scientific activity over the course of sixty-odd years is marked by a number of remarkable discoveries in the physiology of blood circulation, digestion, and trophic functions of the nervous system," he said, occasionally raising his eyes to the ceiling.
The students were frankly bored. Their hands moved automatically across the pages of their notes, rustling their fountain pens and textbooks, but their thoughts were far away from the physiology lecture. The students more often looked out the window, where the spring May sun was playing on the leaves of trees and was reflected in the glass of buildings, rather than listening to the teacher.
At the third desk near the window sat two girls for whom the lecture on physiology was an unbearable torture. In such weather, when the air in the auditorium became heavier and heavier and the

sun generated unbearable stuffiness, they dreamed of the cool waters of the Dnieper, not the halls of the university.

The teacher continued his lecture: "Along with the release of saliva in response to irritation of the oral cavity with food, saliva release in the animal can be achieved on any stimulus of the external world - light, sound, skin irritation, if this stimulus is reinforced by subsequent feeding of the animal ..."

"Viola, believe me, he makes me feel like a real woman!"

Violetta, propping her chin with her left hand, listened attentively to the babble of her groupmate, an appetizing brown-haired girl with a prominent bust. The chatter of her neighbor was much more interesting than the dull lecture.

"Yesterday we were in the restaurant of the hotel "Rus." Did your boyfriend ever invite you to a restaurant?"

"Sure."

"Where have you been?"

"Where? Everywhere. Most often in "Kiev," "Dynamo," "Salute".... He likes those restaurants more than the one in hotel "Rus.""

There was a mixture of disbelief, surprise, and envy on her friend's face.

"Really?"

"He is a very kind and considerate man. He has many friends everywhere."

"Is he studying or working?"

"He's a businessman."

"I fucking dislike all businessmen." - came the voice of a two-meter-tall bodybuilder from behind.

Violetta turned around:

"Don't be bugged, or you'll get a kick in the head!"

The bodybuilder smirked. He, like the girls, was bored.

The bodybuilder fell silent. He was big and strong, with muscles that looked like mountains on his body. But next to Violetta, he always felt small and weak. His heart beat fast when he looked at Violetta. They were groupmates, but to him, Violetta was more than just a friend. Violetta was his dream, his desire, his untold love. He often imagined her naked, making love to her. The bodybuilder loved Violetta, but he couldn't admit it to her. He was too modest, too shy to express his feelings.

Bodybuilder loved her smile, loved her eyes that always shone with joy and kindness. He loved her voice, which always soothed him and excited him at the same time. He wanted to tell her this many times, but he didn't know how to do it. Every time he tried to tell Violetta how he felt, he was overcome with fear. Fear of rejection. Fear of loss. Fear of change. He was afraid of appearing ridiculous in her eyes and in the eyes of his groupmates. Being a vulnerable man, the bodybuilder feared ridicule even more than Violetta's rejection.

Every time he made fun of Violetta during a conversation, the bodybuilder tried to attract her attention.

"Businessmen, at first glance, seem to be businesslike and influential and have money, but as soon as guys of my size come to visit them, they immediately turn from giants into dwarfs and quickly run to the bank for money to pay off the uninvited guests."

Violetta got angry:

"Shut up, you fucking racketeer! My Oleg is not like that! He is not afraid of anyone."

"All business people of today are afraid of something. Some fear the police, and others are afraid of criminals or each other. Trembling with fear for their money, they are ready to betray each other for money. Your boyfriend is just as cowardly as other businessmen."

Brown eyes narrowed with anger. The thin lips are tightly pressed together.

"You really should shut up," her friend intervened, quite pleased that Violetta had been sieged. Of course, she didn't believe that

Violetta's boyfriend took her to pubs almost every day, but she wondered who Violetta's boyfriend was.

The professor nervously tapped his pointer on the chair. The bodybuilder fell silent.

"Experiments have shown that conditioned reflexes are formed on the basis of unconditional ones, providing the best adaptability of the animal to constantly changing environmental conditions," - a monotonous voice floated slowly and sadly over the heads of students.

***

Black plaid shirt. Shorts. Leather belt. Phone call. Gosha's voice in the receiver:

"Khanya, Senya refused to pay."

"Refused to pay? That doesn't sound like Semyon Davydovich."

"We barely got away. There are more cops than there are diners. There's a squad on duty at the entrance all day long."

"I thought Semyon Davydovich would be smarter than that. If you don't want to pay, don't pay, but do it from day one. Lose time, money, health, but don't pay. Once you start paying, you will never quit paying the tribute, no matter what you do."

Pause. Gosha's breathing. Khanya:

"He'd be doing the right thing, though, if he started paying the cops from the beginning rather than after two years under Ahmed's control."

"Shall we wait for the opportune moment and strike?"

"I'm afraid we won't get any more money from this restaurant. All that Senya would have to pay us in the future let him pay to the doctors so that other businessmen would not do such stupid things. This should be a good lesson for everyone. Do you understand me well?"

"Yes, I do."

"You'll do it yourself. Personally. This whole thing is your fault."

"My fault?"
"Whose fault is it? You talked to him, didn't you? You didn't seem to sound very convincing."
"How come? The guys broke the collarbone of a guard from Ahmed's gang in front of everyone outside the cafe."
"The result tells a different story. How's Korotyshka?"
"He's been laid up for two weeks. Got new teeth."
"Take him with you, and don't take too long."
"We'll do it tomorrow or today if we have time."
The receiver goes back to the telephone. A desk. An open book. Heat causing drowsiness. Thoughts lazily flowing. Merging. Going in different directions.

***

How much is a human life worth? Life is priceless. To measure it by money is mean, stupid, impossible, after all! I, like Khanya, had been taught this idea from an early age, and I believed in it. I wish I believed in it now. I don't believe in it because, at the age of thirteen, I knew how much it cost to break an arm, to break the bridge of the nose, to break a jaw, to break a head... Depending on the order and the result (where the person was taken - home or just to the hospital, to the intensive care unit, or to the morgue), the price fluctuated.

"Life is priceless." Years later, when confronted with the concept of "work," I realized why this could not be true. For what does work mean? What does a standardized or irregular working day mean? It is that part of our life that we consciously or unconsciously sell for money so that we use this money to live the rest of our life in a human way (as it is commonly called). The way we want, not the way we are offered. Since we sell ourselves, can it be considered immoral when others sell us to each other?

At the markets, people are perfectly comfortable trading the lives of animals and birds. The fact of trading human life causes us unpleasant feelings because we are still human beings, and it is more difficult to put ourselves in the place of a sold or killed human being than in the place of animals and birds whose meat we eat day by day.

So, how much is life worth? A witty buddy of mine offered me an ingenious formula. Adding up wages for twenty-five years (that is, the entire working life until retirement), we come to the final sum, which is the final and irrevocable price. For example, the salary of a janitor in 1990 was eighty rubles a month. The final amount was equal to twenty-four thousand.

The above formula is very, very conditional. It is clear that no one will kill a janitor for 24 thousand rubles. He would be killed for a glass of vodka, and for a bottle, he would be buried in such a way that even experienced criminalists would not find out where exactly.

In the end, the price of human life is inextricably linked to the social importance of the potential victim. For example, at the turn of the 1990s, devout Muslims around the world searched for the writer Salman Rushdie, author of The Satanic Verses. Muslims found the book offensive and blasphemous. "The Satanic Verses" was banned in Iran, Saudi Arabia, India, Pakistan, and other countries. Iranian leader Ayatollah Ruhollah Khomeini issued a fatwa calling on Muslims around the world to execute those involved in the book. At the same time, an Iranian religious foundation announced a $2 million reward for Rushdie's murder. In 2016, the fee for the writer's murder grew to $4 million.

Strangely enough, for many, the meaning of life emerged. For one, it consisted in the word "survive"; for others - in the word "kill."

In Kiev in May 1990, the fee for work done ranged from five to ten thousand rubles. It is not for nothing they say - "life is priceless"...

***

The anxieties were replaced by serenity. The girl buried her face in Khanya's chest.
"I thought you weren't coming."
They stood at the entrance to the university's red building, where massive columns cut the teeming crowd into thin streams. Their shadows merged into one on the ground. They were together, and they were happy.
"Was I late, or could I not have come?"
Violetta pressed herself even tighter against the boy. His embrace was warm and strong. Next to Khanya Violetta felt safe.
"How long have you been waiting?"
"About two minutes."
He laughed, kissing her face.
"Shall we go?"
"Honey, I can't. We have a meeting at 3:00 in the afternoon. I just found out about it at the last lesson."
"So don't go to the meeting!"
"I promised I would. Believe me, I hate to go, but I have to. I'll call you tonight. Will you be home?"
An affirmative, imperceptible nod of the head.
"I'll meet you tonight, okay? I can't be without you."
A gentle, long kiss. Soft lights in the open brown eyes.

***

Khanya returned to the car alone. Rakhit looked at him in surprise.
"Isn't she coming with us?"
"Violetta has a meeting."
Rakhit laughed:
"Look at her! She still runs to the meetings obediently. Just like a bunny, she hopped back."

The driver breathed a sigh of relief. Rachit felt uncomfortable in her presence. Why? Maybe because Khanya and Violetta were happy with each other. Too happy with each other...

***

"Who was that?" - The bodybuilder asked Violetta.
It was obvious that he was confused.
"Why do you ask?"
"Your boyfriend?"
"Does that surprise you?" - Violetta looked up at her groupmate with a smile.
The bodybuilder cast a tense glance out the open window. At least a gust of wind!
"I imagined him differently."
"Better or worse?"
The playful tone of laughing brown eyes. A long pause in lieu of an answer.
"Viola. I've said a lot of stupid things to you today. I'm sorry, it wasn't out of spite."
Violetta flinched, feeling a sudden coldness touch her heart. The girl fluttered her eyelashes in surprise:
"You didn't hurt me in any way. Why are you apologizing? Did something happen?"
The bodybuilder took his eyes aside. An unpleasant feeling of foreboding encompassed Violetta more and more strongly.
"Nothing happened. Viola, I know this man. A lot of people know him."

***

The coolness of the evening flowed through his body in a wave of relief. The sun was slanting toward the roofs of the distant houses, beyond which lay a thin, string-like horizon line.

The phone didn't ring. Khanya absent-mindedly twirled a fountain pen in his hands, half-sitting in a leather chair at his desk.
Put the pen aside. Closed the notebook and looked at his watch. After a little thought, he picked up the telephone receiver. Dialed a familiar phone number. Long, clear beeps. A familiar voice. A habitually dropped "Yes" at the other end of the telephone wire.
"Letta?"
Silence. Quiet:
"Yes, it's me."
"Did you just get home?"
"No."
A long, drawn-out pause.
"I've been waiting all evening for your call."
"I know."
Khanya shifted the phone receiver from hand to hand.
"Will we meet?"
"I don't think so. I had a change of plans. There's something I have to do."
"Your meeting has long since ended."
"So?"
Telephone wires are like nerves stretched along the walls of houses.
"Anyway, I'll be going to my friend's place via Khreshchatyk."
"Do you need a ride?"
"I'll manage myself. Thank you."
"What time will you be passing through the center?"
"Maybe in an hour and a half."
"Where?"
"I'll be getting off the subway."
"Where did we meet the first time?"
"Yes."
Violetta hung up the phone. She sat down on the sofa with her hands on her knees. She tilted her head to the side, keeping her

eyes on the back of the chair. "I can't live without him, but I can't live with him either."

Violetta had always seen Khanya as a successful businessman. He was handsome, confident, and had a magnetism that attracted people. He was her knight, her hero. But now, this beautiful image shattered into thousands of shards that hurt her heart.

There was no business. Everything was soaked in lies. Khanya had turned out to be the leader of a bloody gang. Violetta felt her breathing become heavy to her as if the air was being sucked out of the room. She tried to picture Khanya skimming tribute from hookers and robbing businessmen, but she couldn't. Violetta couldn't imagine that such a thing was even possible. In her mind, she realized that the real Khanya was a completely different person from the one she had imagined for herself. But in her heart, she could not accept it.

Being a strong-willed person, despite her seeming fragility, Violetta decided to part with Khanya. It was the only right decision she could make. She couldn't be a part of his world. But even with that thought, the ache in her heart did not subside. She still loved him.

Violetta looked at her reflection in the mirror. Her eyes were red with tears, and her face expressed deep pain.

Behind the wall, in the kitchen, her mother was rattling dishes. The door slammed in the hallway - her brother had come home. "Oleg, why do things turn out this way and not the other way round?" In an hour and a half, the disk of the glowing sun would disappear behind the horizon line. "Can't it be otherwise?"

"It can't," Letta thought as a wheeze escaped from the inflamed lungs of a city of many millions.

***

"You can drive me to Khreshchatyk."

Rakhit was fiddling with the engine.

"I hate that place. Thieves, cops, and brokers mixed with homeless people."

The driver got even deeper into the BMW's innards.

"Stop grumbling. We have to go."

Rakhit wiped the sweat off his forehead:

"We should go. But the car won't start. I'll go to the service station on Monday."

Khanya looked at his watch impatiently:

"Repair it. I'll go."

Rakhit, covered with mud and oil, poked his head out.

"Wait for about twenty minutes. What's the hurry? There's nothing urgent today."

"You don't have any. I do."

Rakhit said, "I wouldn't advise you to go there alone."

Khanya flared up:

"Since when are you going to give me advice?"

"It's up to you..."

Rakhit leaned over the engine again. He was about to say something else. He turned around. Khanya got into a cab and drove away.

***

In tight-fitting jeans and a loose blue T-shirt, Violetta strode out into the street. Her graceful, fragile figure stood out sharply against the faceless mass of passersby. Frowning slightly, the girl with luxurious brown hair looked around. Strong arms encircled her from behind by her flexible waist, and hot lips touched the hair on the back of her neck. Abruptly turning around, the girl wrapped her arms around his neck and pulled the man to her. A moment later, she recoiled.

"I've been told everything about you!"

In response, an attentive look, a smile.

"What's so funny?"
His brown eyes were wide open like two bottomless wells turned toward the clear light of Heaven.
"Even I don't know everything about myself. Besides, I don't tell others about my affairs."
"You don't trust anyone!"
"Why should I? Everyone should know only what they need to know. It's bad for friends and enemies alike to know too much."
"I understand enemies, but friends? Why?"
"They don't need to worry unnecessarily, stay awake at night, swallow valerian. Anxiety in excessive doses shortens their lifespan. It's already short. According to statistics."
The sound of leaves in the famous chestnut alley above their heads.
"You said you work in a company."
"I work in an unregistered company. We pay no taxes to the state and receive no subsidies. We have no one to rely on but ourselves."
"You have everything - money, apartment, car, friends... Everything you need to live. Why would you risk it by crossing the line every day?"
"I don't think I have it all. That's one thing. Second of all, I got all those things you mentioned by crossing a line. The minute I turn back, not go, just turn, I lose everything. It's not just friends."
"You're taking tribute from co-ops and hookers! You're robbing people. It's immoral!"
"We only take money from those who have profited at the expense of others, and we don't touch those who work for a single wage. As for trading women's bodies, that's not really our specialty. We only tax those who put them on the street."
"What a Robin Hood! I bet you've been going to and sleeping with various girls after me."
"Is that jealousy?"

The girl burst into flames. He guessed.
"I have no reason to be jealous of you because I don't intend to see you again."
The glare of the sunset reflected in his eyes with the glow of red-hot metal.
"Are you unhappy with me?" - he asked the girl quietly.
"No..." - Violetta answered as quietly as if someone was listening. – "Fool, I fell in love with you ..."
"What's changed since some asshole said all those things about me? Have I changed?"
Violetta thought about it.
"I can't live with a criminal."
"Morals are strong," Khanya grinned wryly. – "What do you know about me, and on what basis do you dare to judge me? Yes, I don't live by the laws of the state I was born and raised in, but I'm not a criminal. Can't you see that it's impossible to live by the laws of our country? Some laws contradict others, and some are meaningless. What they have in common is that they are all aimed at destroying the slightest expression of individuality in a person. Just because we breathe, we can already be sent to jail - there will always be a reason. Being an individual is the worst crime in this society. Universal equality of equally thinking individuals is the ideal of the society we live in. Poverty is encouraged as much as wealth is reviled. The government shuns private property like a venereal disease, and it is foolish to expect it to change for the better.

I know there are worse and better countries in the world than ours, but I didn't have to choose where I was born. Whether we want it or not, we are a part of this earth, but I do not want to be a part of this society. That's why I created my own world and live by my own fairer laws.

Don't be in a hurry to judge. Don't be in a hurry to leave. After all, it's so easy to turn around, walk away..."

A light twilight gust of wind touched her black hair. Violetta didn't know what to say. His voice had a magical effect on the girl. She wanted to go to him and realized that if she didn't leave now, she would never leave.

'I have to go.' - The timid touch of his hands. – 'Don't call me again. Okay?"

Khanya was silent. The girl slowly lowered her head. Just as slowly, she stepped back. The more Violetta wanted to stay, the faster she left, almost running along Khreshchatyk, the main artery of the city. She disappeared and then appeared in the crowd of people.

Hold out your hand! Stop her if you can! One more moment, and maybe it would be too late....

Khanya rushed after Violetta. A sharp honk made him look back. A familiar BMW pulled up to the trolley bus stop. Rakhit's sickly pale face broke into a silly smile. Gosha got out of the car, followed by a slimmed-down Korotyshka. They had done a good job today and were pleased with themselves.

Khanya looked after Violetta once more. He was losing her, and he was in unbearable pain. A moment more and the fragile figure disappeared into the waves of the river of people. Only now did he realize the distance between them. Another world was calling Khanya, another life in which he chose himself.

PART II

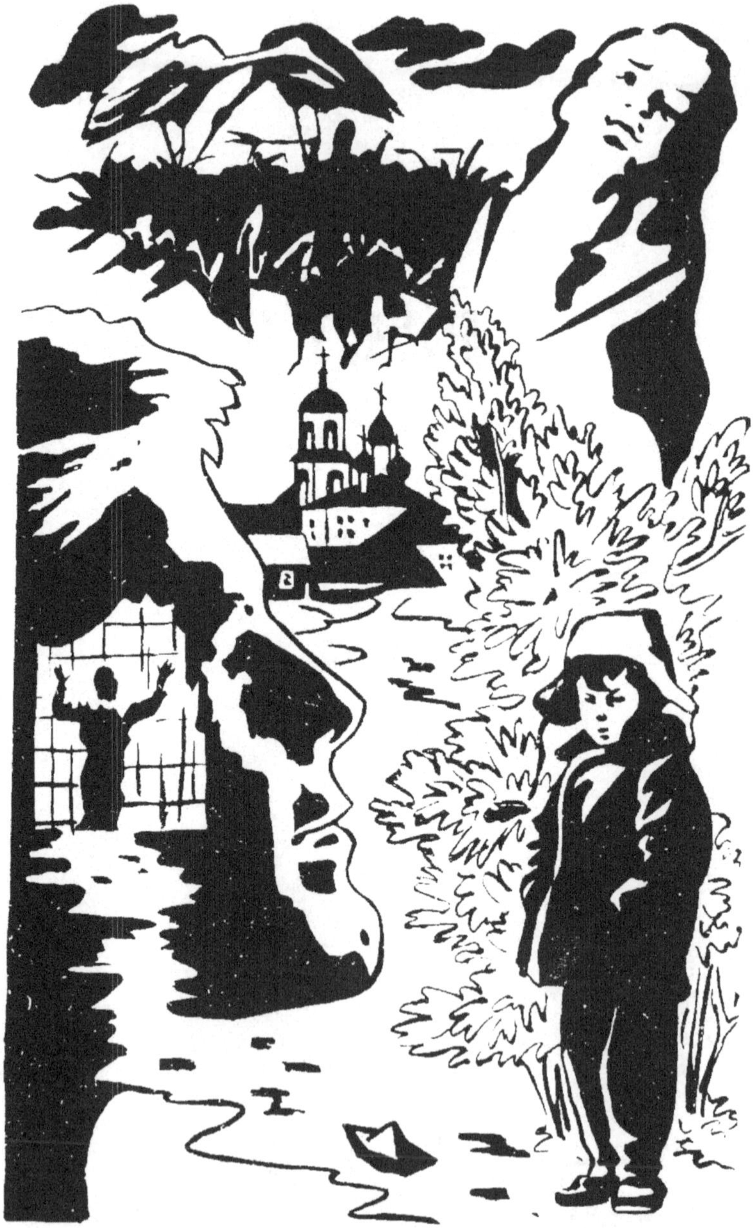

CHAPTER I

Having thrown off his army tunic with the epaulets of a senior sergeant of anti-aircraft missile forces, Oleg Khanin stretched out on the shelf of a double compartment in a sleeping carriage, yawning contentedly. An hour ago, no one could guarantee that he would be able to get on the train, tickets for which were sold out long ago. No wonder, the October holidays were ahead.

On the road leading to Kiev, he was always lucky. His whole being was eager to get home after two years' separation, dreading the stoppages on the way more than anything else. He felt it clearly in Kharkov when he was told at the window of the railroad ticket office: "There are no tickets, and there will be none."

At such a concrete statement of the problem, some people became despondent, looking in advance for a place to spend the night near the walls of the gray station building. Others began to argue loudly with the cashier. As if it might help to get the seats.

Khanin belonged to the third group. Those who having heard the words "No seats," calmly went and took the seats they wanted, leaving their anger and discontent to the first two categories of citizens.

It happened likewise this time. Waiting for the moment when the conductor hesitated at the door, Oleg's shadow slipped into the depths of the first carriage. Only when the train moved and Kharkov remained far behind, Oleg approached the conductor with a guilty, open smile. Twenty-five rubles quickly settled the matter. The carriage turned out to be a sleeping car, and the compartment was a two-seater without a traveling companion. There were sixty rubles and change in his shirt's breast pocket. For a guy who received about seven rubles a month for two army years, it was a lot of money.

Oleg was happy. He was going home! He looked outside the window, into the darkness, passing lantern lights, silhouettes of houses. The words of a familiar song were ringing in his ears: "The wheels are banging merrily, I am no longer a soldier ..." How long had he waited for this fall - the fall of 1985.

***

Kiev met Oleg with the cold of autumn, yellow leaves floating drearily between the tops of trees and the dreary frozen ground. The guy with a short soldier's hairstyle was strolling along Khreshchatyk. The smiles of all the girls he met seemed directed at him alone. The variegated colors were streaming brightly into his eyes, blinding him. It was unusual for him to see the variety of colors. Only two colors accompanied him in the army - green and gray. Green - the color of uniforms, the color of the military, the color of the grass behind the barbed wire of army units. Gray - the color of life of the armed forces, the color of the platform, the color of the sky above his head. Walking in the crowd, Oleg reveled in freedom. He did not think yet about how to go on living. Questions still needed to line up in a cold row. The feeling of anxiety did not envelop his thoughts. What lies ahead? Oleg will ask himself about it a bit later.

***

As a child, Oleg grew quiet and withdrawn in his world. Other children rarely entered his world which was invisible to outsiders. His parents, who had enrolled their son in the kindergarten, had to take him back after a week and a half. The child organically did not tolerate preschool institutions. As soon as the parents left, the rosy-cheeked baby would silently lie down on the floor, refusing to eat, and would lie there until angry parents arrived and took the child home with a scandal. Neither persuasion nor threats helped. The child was ready to give up his favorite toys to avoid attending the kindergarten he hated! In the end, the parents capitulated.

Thus, Oleg won the first battle in his life - the battle for the right not to go where he did not want.

The son was satisfied, the parents - not. The question arose: what to do with him, where to stay from eight in the morning till six in the evening. Leave him at home? That's not a solution. Little children should spend as much time as possible in the fresh air.

Opposite the house, there was a rectangular public garden. Every morning at eight o'clock, Oleg was brought to this garden and left to walk alone. At one o'clock in the afternoon, his mother would come home from work, feed the child, and send him out again. At six o'clock in the evening, the father would pick up his son on his way back from work. Such an unconventional solution to the problem surprised the neighbors and angered the relatives.

"How can you leave a child alone in the street?" – people asked Oleg's mother with indignation.

"We agreed with my son that he would not go outside the park. Nothing can happen to him. He is an adult and quite an independent person."

"Outrageous!" - The relatives wouldn't stop. Everyone was indignant, but none of them offered their help to look after the "adult and quite independent person," who was barely four years old at that time.

Stuffing his chubby hands into the pockets of his pants, Oleg walked around, left to himself. He knew that at any moment, he could go beyond the garden but did not abuse his mother's trust. He was trusted, for he was an adult! That's what the little boy thought. How could he not? After all, he had such freedom of choice which none of his peers living nearby had.

Oleg walked alone in the park for three years. To study birds, consider dogs, watch people - all this brought real pleasure. What could be more beautiful than learning about the world? A vast, mysterious world that holds so many riddles and secrets! How he wanted to grow up quickly and learn everything that adults knew...

It was a long time ago that his childhood passed. External events that happened to Oleg during those distant three childhood years disappeared from memory. However, that feeling of boundless freedom remained in him for the rest of his life.

***

At school Oleg could not tolerate its dogmatism and unspeakable boredom. He was also annoyed with his dull classmates. Oleg was far ahead of them in development, material, and spiritual needs. As for the older guys, they had their own interests, their own circle, in which the kids like Oleg were not allowed. However, the kid did not seek their companionship. The colossal library, left as an inheritance from his grandfather, was astonishing in size, surprising in variety, captivating with bright old bindings, shining with gilt and silver. Returning home after school, Oleg threw his rucksackwith textbooks in the far corner of the hallway, closed his room, and plunged into reading his favorite books. The child's mind intricately absorbed Andersen's fairy tales and visions of Edgar Poe, later - the pessimism of Schopenhauer and the soft irony of Oscar Wilde. There were a lot of things Oleg did not and could not understand due to his age and lack of life experience. Confusing, vague, and unknowable things attracted him like a clever crossword puzzle, which (he believed) he would solve someday.

***

One of Oleg's classmates liked to twist surnames and give nicknames in every possible way. Thus, Kozlovetsky quickly turned into Kozel, Kapustyansky into Kapusta, and Khanin got three nicknames at once: Sullen River, Zanuda, and Khanya. The first two were somehow left out by themselves, but Khanya stuck, as it turned out, for a long time.

Oleg could not stand it when someone twisted his last name. This fact humiliated him and caused a sense of protest and irritation. Remaining outwardly calm and friendly to others, Oleg vowed not to forget the offense and remind it someday.

The case presented itself a few years later - in either sixth or seventh class. Anton, a so-called classmate, sat on the windowsill with his legs hanging down and talked to a friend standing on the sports field in front of the school. Oleg entered the classroom and habitually put his briefcase on the desk. Wanted to sit down and then noticed that besides him and Anton, there was no one else in the botany classroom. The classmate was engrossed in the conversation and did not see Oleg. Khanya slowly approached the window and looked around several times - the classroom was empty. A sharp jolt. Oleg dashed to the door, caught his breath, left the classroom, and went downstairs to the dining room.

On the street – bustle, shouts. Ambulance. Voices:

"What's wrong with him? Did he fall?"

"He fell from the third floor."

"I saw..."

The irritated voice of a man in a white coat:

"Make way. Make way!"

"Broke his leg. Oh, my God! Look, there's blood on his head."

"It's good he's alive. You'd better watch the kids instead of crying over them. Let me through!"

More yelling.

At the next lesson in all classes, teachers strictly forbade students to sit on the windowsills. They explained what sloppiness and carelessness can lead to! (After two days, the ban was safely forgotten.) The idea that Anton could have been pushed and one of the students had a chance to become a murderer, did not cross anyone's mind. And Anton himself, because of the shock, did not understand how the boy happened to fall out of the window.

Oleg sat melancholically at his desk, propped his chin with his fist, not paying attention to the bustle around him. Feverishly beating thought: "Why? Why did I do that?" Only having recalled the offense and the promise of revenge, he sighed in relief, gazing at the leaves of the trees outside the half-closed window. Tension was replaced by satisfaction at what he had done. He might have forgotten what he'd promised himself years ago, but he hadn't. He had kept his word!

***

In childhood, in school years especially, each of us had conflicts and ordinary childhood fights. Some of us had them rarely, others daily. We hurt people, and people hurt us. The interaction of these two types of pain shaped our character, attitude to the world, and ourselves ... That day, when Oleg pushed Anton out of the window, he did not think about the pain he brought into someone else's life. For himself Khanya solved this question much earlier. In winter, when he was only about five years old.

***

It was a beautiful winter day. Frost and sunshine. Just like in Pushkin's poem. Near Khanya's house, children were sledding down the hill. Oleg looked enviously out the window at his peers, then took the sled and went outside with his mother.
"Olezhek, you'll get cold - run home."
"Why do parents like to sit at home on Sundays?" - the kid was looking at his mom in surprise.
Oleg sat down on the sled and drove down the hill once, twice ... Sparks of snow and ice glistered brightly in the sun. Snowflakes fell on his face, turning into clear, transparent water droplets.
"Let me ride!"
Strong hands roughly snatched the sled. A sturdy boy of about eight in a sports cap confidently sat on Oleg's sled and rushed

down the hill with a joyful shout, paying no attention to the kid who was flapping his eyelashes offendedly. The good mood was gone.
A few minutes later, Oleg approached the tough boy.
"Give it back!"
"Get away, little one ..."
The hardy boy rolled merrily down.
What to do? The eight-year-old was clearly stronger.
Oleg noticed that all the children descended on the sled on the same rolled track. Fifty feet from the top of the hill, the rut was near a high-voltage box. After thinking for a second or two, Khanya went down thirty feet from the top.
The hardy boy no longer remembered exactly from whom he had taken the sled. Did it matter? The mood was wonderful. Once again (for the second time!), having climbed the hill, the boy laid down on the sled with his belly. He pushed off the snow with his hands and rushed down the sparkling snow.
As soon as the sled aligned with Oleg, he sharply pushed them with his foot. It didn't take much force to change the direction a little. After flying a few feet, the sled crashed into a brick wall. The boy jumped up and ran down the street like a stung man, holding the palm of his right hand to his head. His blood-stained sports cap remained lying on the snow.
Oleg took his sled. He did not ride anymore - the mood was finally broken. Khanya looked after the fleeing eight-year-old, then at the cap lying on the snow. The bold, arrogant tone and the pathetic, fear-filled cry - all in one person.
What had changed the moment he hit the brick wall?
After checking if he had lost his mittens, Oleg silently headed toward the home, dragging the sled behind him on a rope. A scream was ringing in his ears. Droplets of blood. Snow - white and pure. A sports cap. Pain. What is pain?

***

The school years passed imperceptibly. Everyone started the tenth grade with a firm intention to pore over their textbooks earnestly and apply to higher educational institutions upon graduation. Many vowed to themselves and others that during the last year of study they would grow wiser. The enthusiasm lasted for two months. By winter, the majority had safely forgotten about the bright impulses to study and only study. The minority continued to pore over their textbooks. Khanya remained among the minority. By the beginning of March, no one had any doubts that he would finish school with "honours" and enter the history department of the university. Secretly, Oleg was proud: he managed to drive himself into the rigid limits of the regime. Weekdays flowed imperceptibly into weekends, weekends - into weekdays. Nothing broke the usual course of life. There seemed to be no force that could change once and for all the established rhythm. But...

With an unconscious movement, the textbooks were pushed aside as well as the rigid rhythm and plans for the future. An instant changed the usual course of the days. Lena entered Khanya's life. She entered it swiftly, easily, and confidently without asking either permission or advice.

***

It happened at noon on March 8. Oleg was returning home from Bessarabsky market with a lovely bouquet of roses as a present for his mother. His thoughts were hovering somewhere far away - in a labyrinth of mathematical and chemical formulas - and suddenly came to earth. The festive mood of passers-by, bouquets of roses in their hands, silver snow, bright sunshine. Oleg felt sad and lonely. Apart from relatives, teachers, and acquaintances, he had no one to greet on the holiday. An unconscious desire, suppressed by an effort of will in the depths of the self, bursts out of the hidden depths of the subconscious.

Lena flitted out of the underground passage. Her blond fluffy hair was scattered on her bright blue jacket. Half-closing her eyes from the dazzling rays of the spring sun, the girl with a light movement threw back her unruly bang.

"Let me greet you on the International Women's Day!

At first, Lena did not realize it was addressed to her. A shy smile on the guy's face.

"This is for you." - A huge bouquet in his outstretched hand.

"For me?" - The girl smiled and looked straight into his eyes.

"Can I meet you somewhere?"

"Try."

"I'll call?"

The girl laughed:

"Call."

A short conversation. A few numbers were hastily written down on a scrap of paper.

***

Who was Lena to him? A vague image from his childhood dreams. The touch of a dream. The hot breath of sunset on the threshold of evening twilight. Falling into the bottomless abyss of the universe. The glow of distant, unexplored stars. Lena didn't know how to love halfway. She either loved or she didn't. The girl didn't need the bright colors of tomorrow. To turn today into an endless time interval, to slow down the movement of hands on the clock face, to stop the transience of moments, enjoying the closeness of a loved one - in her understanding, this was the meaning of happiness.

People tend to give up real benefits for the sake of illusory ones. All of us are often looking for something we cannot obtain. Maybe this is due to the fact that the meaning of existence is not in achieving the goal but in the pursuit of it, in moving along the chosen path?

Oleg conducted several experiments with other girls a year and a half later. "If I feel good with Lena - then I should be good with other women," thought Oleg. He began to look for what he already had, not thinking about the fact that it was easy to lose and difficult to find.

The girl first felt the crack when during their dates, Oleg suddenly cut off the phrase on the half-word, staring pensive look somewhere in the distance, where the pale rays of the moon disk broke on the cold waves of the Dnieper.

They parted without loud words and mutual reproaches. They simply began to date less and less often, and then they stopped seeing each other altogether.

"I'm going to the army," - Oleg once said, finishing a glass of orange juice.

Lena lifted herself off the bed. Her blond hair touched her chest.

"Two years. How long... I'll wait for you."

"Why? Two years will change us. We'll be different. In that time, you'll meet someone better than me."

"I don't need better."

"It's not worth ruining your life."

Lena put her head down on the pillow. Turned away. Oleg thought at the time that he acted honorably.

***

Khanya left for the army in November 1983. The day before, he got up at six in the morning, leisurely swallowed his breakfast, threw his backpack with a change of underwear over his shoulder, and went to the military enlistment office. Deep in his heart he hoped to serve in Ukraine, but in Kharkiv they were put on the Volgograd train and then sent to Astrakhan. Oleg realized that he would not serve in his homeland.

The army resembled a dumping ground for intellectual garbage. Oleg finally confirmed the idea that only those who are not capable of anything more enter military schools. Complete jerks, who could not reach the officer ranks, went to become ensigns.

***

On the first day, the sergeant tugged Khanya's sleeve:
"Clean the toilet. Make it sparkle! I'll check in ten minutes. Time's up!"
Oleg glared at his peer. The usual snob. Like those whom he used to beat in the schoolyard.
"If you need, then you clean the toilet."
The sergeant's eyes widened in surprise.
"What?! I'm gonna kill you!"
"Try it."
"I'll..."
The sergeant ran down the stairs. "Where has he gone so fast?" - Oleg did not understand at first, but he immediately realized when he saw a familiar uniform, accompanied by a red-haired sergeant larger in the shoulders. Doubts about the intentions of the redhead did not arise.
"Are you getting impudent?" - The question sounded from the top step of the stairwell. Not thinking long, Oleg responded with a fist on the open mouth:
"Yes, it's me."
The redhead rolled down the stairs, knocking down two soldiers who were climbing the stairs.
The whole company ran to the noise. Soldiers and sergeants in the front. New recruits like Oleg were watching with interest to see what would happen. Khanya glared at the others, feeling the blood boiling in his veins.
The senior sergeant of the battalion, a tall sergeant with a mustache, came up to Oleg.

He looked carefully into his eyes and suddenly smiled:
"Do you think such things are easy to get away with?"
A big brute in a dirty, slippery uniform tried to get Khanya with a boot between his legs, but the mustachioed man held him back:
"Not now. We'll talk after lights out."
And he smiled again, just as suddenly and calmly. The brute somehow immediately softened and stepped aside.
"They won't forgive," - whispered the recruit lying on the neighboring bed after the evening inspection. – "They'll take you to the storeroom and..."
"Sleep!"
A sharp shout from the night sergeant on battalion duty. The recruits obediently ducked under the blankets. Khanya alone remained seated on the bed. The sergeant wanted to say something, then changed his mind. Jingling his keys, he wandered toward the armory.
At half past twelve, Oleg was called to the Lenin room. The cramped room could accommodate twenty people. Oleg stopped at the map of the USSR. In the pocket of his pants lay a screwdriver prepared in advance.
On a chair by the door sat the redhead. Evidently, the Muscovite had lost his top two teeth. Wrapping his belt around his right hand, a Caucasian-looking big man - one of those who had only a few days left to serve - slid off the lid.
"You raised your hand on the sergeant, puppy...?"
Oleg did not take his eyes off him. "Well, hit me first, hit me..." - the thought was pulsing in his head. The belt buckle, like boiling hot water, burned his left cheek. Oleg recoiled, convulsively throwing forward his right hand. The screwdriver pierced the notebook and military ID card in the man's left breast pocket, scratching the skin only slightly. The Caucasian shrieked and bounced away, clutching his chest near his heart. Seeing nothing in front of him, Oleg slashed the screwdriver through the air.

"Relax."

What a strange voice. The tall sergeant with a mustache stood in front of him.

"If you want to stab someone, stab me first."

The blood rushed from his face. Reason slowly returned to Oleg.

"Screwdriver!"

Instinctively, like a machine, Oleg unclenched his hand.

"Everyone to sleep."

The voice is confident, calm, and authoritative. Disobedience is impossible. Sergeants headed for the door.

"If I order - you will wash everything. Understand?"

"No," - Oleg mentally answered, but the voice from within ordered, called. A hitherto unfamiliar will made Oleg nod his head obediently.

"That would be better."

The tall sergeant sat down on the edge of the table:

"Tell me where you came from."

***

The tall sergeant's name was Andrey Zakharchenko. This strange man, withdrawn in himself and not understood by anyone, remained in Oleg's memory for life. Andrey had an amazing gift to suppress someone else's will like snakes paralyze frogs with a look before eating them. The tall sergeant was first talked about when he was still a simple private with a month's army experience. During training firing, all the bullets from Andrey's gun hit exactly the center of the target.

Commanders disliked the guy, although they were impressed by his desire for order and the ability to manage his fellow soldiers. Soon, Zakharchenko was promoted to sergeant and commander of the squad, then petty officer. Over time, his company turned into an exemplary mindless machine, subject to a truly diabolical, unsolved will.

Andrey did not receive letters from home and did not write himself. He had no friends as such. Khanya was the only one whom Andrey brought close to him. Thanks to Zakharchenko, Oleg was never given dirty, hard work, but they could not be called friends. Oleg knew nothing about Andrey's past. All conversations were reduced to nothing. Zakharchenko liked listening and did not like talking.

"Tomorrow I go home," one day in the fall of 1984, Andrey broke mundanely, carefully ironed his parade-exit uniform after the all clear signal. "Don't be sad, Oleg. You see for yourself: time flies by. Soon, it will be your turn."

It was strange how he said those words: "Soon it will be your turn." The night passed as usual. Early in the morning, without saying a word to anyone, Andrey took a Kalashnikov gun from the weapons room and went out into the yard. He squatted down taking a long look at the birds soaring high in the sky. Then he shot himself in the head. There were no letters or notes left after him.

***

Memories swirled over his head like tired autumn leaves. Oleg walked along Khreshchatyk. Separate episodes flashed brightly in his memory, layered on top of each other, fading, framed by bitterness and warmth. Service in the army cut life into two parts. One part remained beyond the "before" line, and the second part - beyond the "after" line - was just beginning.

CHAPTER II

Khanya's grandmother left her grandson an apartment in Obolon as an inheritance. When Oleg returned from the army, he could not understand (and never did) his own feelings - whether he was saddened by the death of his grandmother, whom he did not even know, or whether he was happy because he had his own apartment! It was not easy to get your own housing in the Soviet Union.

His parents secretly breathed a sigh of relief when their son started living on his own. They considered themselves relatively young and wanted to live in their own time.

"Are you sure we did the right thing by moving your son out?" Khanya's father was worried.

"You'll see, he'll marry soon and have a family of his own. Let him make his own future."

His mother was optimistic.

"He's not the kind of man who gets married in a hurry," - his father said in a low voice.

"Today, he is in no hurry, but tomorrow, he will meet a girl and fall in love with her. Today's generation is not like ours. They do everything quickly."

That was the end of the discussion.

***

In the beginning, Oleg drank a lot of alcohol with his friends and housemates, overwhelmed by the boundless freedom beyond his control. He was a hospitable host and quickly made friends with his housemates. There were people with criminal backgrounds among them.

When he got bored with the parties, Oleg thought about work. Khanya was well aware of the fact that finding something high-paid would not be easy. He did not have the appropriate education. So, Khanya began to look for a simple, not heavy job, even if it was not well paid, so that to start somewhere.

One day, an advertisement, "A cleaner is required," caught his eye. It was an inconspicuous ad on a rusty metal panel. Sweeping the streets? Shoveling shit out of garbage cans? Oleg had never done such work, and he was sure that he would not do it. And yet there was something in this announcement. Oleg could not understand what exactly attracted him to this announcement. After hesitating for a minute, he went to the Human Resources department.

Turning from an ordinary citizen to an ordinary cleaner with a salary of eighty rubles was not so easy. For two days Oleg had been undergoing a medical examination: had a fluorography taken, was examined by a surgeon, ophthalmologist, and dermatologist, did blood count. Then he filled out a pile of papers.

"Can I ask?" - Oleg asked. – "If it suddenly turns out that one of my distant relatives accidentally ended up in German captivity forty years ago, will I be dismissed immediately or later?"

"Fill out the application form, and do not ask stupid questions!" - snapped the blond lady with sparrow eyes over painted cheeks.

Oleg obeyed. The next morning, he went to work. To sweep the asphalt and clean the urns were not the things he was intended to do. With a broom, he wandered around the territory of the enterprise, watching what was going on around him and what his colleagues were doing at the beginning of the working day.

The coworkers were asleep. The janitorial staff was a pathetic rabble. Unshaven, in chewed-up clothes, they were often drunk.

Oleg managed to make a deal with them quite quickly. For two bottles of vodka and food, Khanya's lot was cleaned regularly. Thus, Oleg solved the problem of employment, at least at the initial stage.

Having worked for a few months, Oleg learned the truth well: the ability to organize the work of others brings much more money than working for someone. If you understand it, there are opportunities to earn as much as you want. The whole question is how to realize these opportunities. Whoever finds the answer to that question gets a chance. Even if it's a small chance, it's still a chance.

***

The doorbell rang. Annoying and long. A sip of mineral water. Oleg lifted himself off the sofa without hurrying.
"It's good I caught you at home," - the neighbor entered the apartment.
"What do you want? I'm asleep?" - Oleg asked.
"In the daytime? We've known each other for a long time." The guest began.
He lived in the neighboring entrance. Some time ago – that was about three months since Oleg moved to a new apartment – they met by chance, as they usually got acquainted with neighbors in the house. He knew that Oleg lived alone and once came to visit him with a bottle of cognac. That was all about the acquaintance.
"I'll be honest with you."
Judging by the running eyes and fat chin, the neighbor did not belong to the category of "sincere people".
"My friend is coming. It's expensive to put him in a hotel, and I don't have enough room in my apartment."
Oleg indifferently listened to the neighbor.
"Maybe he'll stay with you? You still live alone."
The neighbor looked into Oleg's eyes.
"For you, he's a friend, but for me, he's a stranger." Khanya answered.
"Why do you say that? He's a cool guy, I guarantee it! And he'll pay. You need money."
Oleg thought. On the one hand, he didn't need a stranger, but on the other hand, he needed money. Khanya lived alone in the apartment.

***

The neighbor's friend, about forty years old, with a face like a fattened piglet and eyes as smart as an anthill, carefully placed a bright sports bag with the inscription "Puma" on a stool.
"Alexei," the guest introduced himself.
"What could they have in common?" - was the first thought that ran through Oleg's mind. The neighbor ingratiatingly ran around the solidly built figure of his friend, who was about one meter ninety tall, until Lesha, with an open smile, rattled on:
"Go away. I'm fed up with you."
The neighbor coughed and disappeared behind the door.

***

Alexei turned out to be an unusually calm, balanced man. As a rule, he slept during the day. He watched TV regularly. He read the Bible. He rarely left the house. Every morning, he would go grocery shopping at the supermarket in his tracksuit, then go to bed and sleep until late afternoon. From evening till morning, he wandered silently around the apartment, carried weights, and made a lot of calls to different cities. After each call, he carefully put the money by the telephone set.
Moscow, Leningrad, Kazan, Yerevan, Vladikavkaz... The cities changed like in a colorful kaleidoscope. An unusual way of life, the abundance of calls to different cities and republics, lack of information about where he took money from - all this spoke about the extraordinary personality of the guest.
Oleg did not ask anything; he believed that everyone has the right to live as he sees fit. Alexei appreciated Khanya's ability not to ask unnecessary questions. Several weeks passed. The guest was not going to leave Kiev.

***

Leningrad has very cold winters. On January 17, 1982, Alexei ran from Leningrad across Russia in a homemade terrycloth robe after jumping from a third-floor window into a snowdrift below. It wasn't about the love of thrills. In another situation, Alexei wouldn't leave the house even from the first floor in such cold weather.

To better understand Alexei's condition in those days, one should mentally go back to the autumn of 1984, when several large organizations of the city of Leningrad were robbed on the same day.

Who knows, things may have changed nowadays, but in the mid-eighties of the last century, money was not always transported by armed security collectors. On payday, money for stores and factories was transported with guards, but money for institutions such as secondary schools was transported without guards. No one thought about the fact that an ordinary organization located in an old building could receive huge sums of money for their employees' salaries. As a rule, it was the accountant who went after the money. Sometimes, the director of the organization would provide the accountant with one or two workers to help carry the bags of money. Those were not security guards, and they were not responsible for the safety of the money.

I always wondered why thieves rarely took advantage of such carelessness? Is it because robbing small businesses in those years was disreputable and humiliating?

Alexei bet on basic negligence, and he was right. For two months, he spied on cashiers and collectors from various organizations and studied the structure and activities of twenty-three enterprises. In the end, he selected four possibilities. Twelve people and four cars were needed for the robbery. Selecting people for the robbery, Alexei was helped by Zosik - his old friend with whom they had been in prison together.

Polish poet Stanisław Jerzy Lec wrote that the mother of crime is stupid, but its fathers are often brilliant. Everything was carefully thought out: the robbery was successful, and the money in the amount of 2,473,286 rubles was stolen. They decided to divide the money not immediately but later after the noise subsided. Two people knew exactly where the money was hidden: Zosik and Alexei.

On December 8, 1984, Zosik disappeared. Few people would pay attention to this because Zosik had often been drinking and out of touch before. But Alexei got worried:

"No one knows where the money is but Zosik. He should not disappear for a long time."

No one was particularly worried about one-hundred-kilogram Zosik, whose chest and back were adorned with prison tattoos. However, the days went by, and Zosik did not show up. Many people thought that Zosik had run away with the money.

During that time, the Leningrad police were looking for criminals. They couldn't find anything or anyone. However, the robbers were not going to hide anywhere. None of them left the city and they did not try to hide. Furious with anger, the criminals were looking for a former friend. The interests of the criminal world and the police coincided. Everyone was looking for the stolen money.

Zosik was found by a couple of students in love. The half-decomposed corpse was fished out of the Neva River and identified by tattoos. For the police, there was a new mystery, and the criminals had new questions. And those questions were directed at Alexei. He was the only one who was obliged to know where the money was, and in this case, only he benefited from Zosik's death.

A well-known thief who had a high position in the criminal hierarchy had to flee from Leningrad, miraculously saving his life. You can hide from the police. It's harder to hide from your enemies. They have more serious reasons to search. But how can you hide from those who yesterday were your close friends? They know all the back roads. Cut off from the outside world, Alexei frantically tried to remember the acquaintances he hadn't seen for over ten years and who could hide him. Clutching his temples with his hands, Alexei tensely thought in the smoky coupe of the train Leningrad - Rostov-on-Don. In the morning - a king; in the evening - a beggar. What was ahead of him?

***

One day, Khanya found Alexei in a good mood after returning home.
"Oleg, where have you been walking all day?" - A friendly clap on the shoulder.
"Good news, and look who brought it to me!"
Oleg looked into the room, expecting to see a man like Alexei.
"Olya," - blushing, exhaled a fragile girl wrapped in a blanket.
"I'm going home today."
Alexei spoke without ceasing. For the first time in a month and a half, Oleg saw the guest so talkative.
"It's been so many years since I left Leningrad, and I still can't get used to it. It's my city, you know, my city."
"The Summer Garden, the Winter Palace, Nevsky... I've heard a lot, but I've never been there."
Alexei laughed:
"You have heard? You have to see Leningrad. You have to live in it and breathe the air of this city to realize that Leningrad is Leningrad. It is the ancient capital of Russia."
"And Moscow?"
"What about Moscow? There are no real Russians in Moscow anymore. A mixture of Slavs, Asians, and Jews. But I admit that there's much money to make in Moscow."
Alexei always believed he was born under a lucky star. Not having the slightest chance, he believed that he would someday return to

his hometown. Olya brought the annulment of his death sentence to Kiev.

The money, rotted by damp and eaten by rats, was found in the attic of Zosik's house. This meant that Alexei was acquitted and was not guilty of either Zosik's death or disappearance of the money. Also, Alexei had the right to demand compensation for moral damage from the criminal community of Leningrad. He was accused in vain.

However, some said it was a skillful staging on Alexei's instructions: it was impossible to determine how much money was originally there. It was also unknown who had killed Zosik and why.

***

Kiev. Airport. Forty minutes left before the flight.
"Take the rent for the apartment," Alexei held out the money.
"No need. We're friends."
"Take it. I know you need the money."
Alexei slipped the money into Oleg's pocket. Then he added after a brief pause.
"You have good personal qualities, Oleg, and many guys are hanging around you. But you live far below your abilities. For nothing."
"There was no one to advise."
"Now there will be. Believe me, I know people well enough. And I do not forget those who I appreciate."
Oleg looked sadly at Alexei leaving. He got used to his strange guest.
"I do not know whether we will see each other in the future or not."
"We will see each other. Don't doubt it."
A feeling of inexplicable anxiety seized Oleg as he saw him going away. His intuition told Khanya that something was going to

happen in the near future between him and Alexei, but he didn't understand what it might be.

Carelessly placing her hand on Alexei's shoulder Olya walked toward the plane with the easy, graceful gait of a satisfied female who had grabbed her prey. Slender fingers spiderwebbed the base of his neck.

***

The spring wind dispelled the tense atmosphere created by Alexei after the door slammed shut behind him. There were no more endless calls all over the Soviet Union, no more long conversations about nothing and, at the same time, about everything in the world, that lasted far after midnight.

The everyday life went on in the streets of evening Kiev, indifferently equating yesterday, today, and tomorrow.

Oleg shook his head. He did not want to live like others, to rot alive in the four walls of the apartment and, once a month, to buy someone sausage and vodka. Khanya aspired to live a different life, where beautiful women appreciate strength and intelligence, and men are courageous and honest. Is there such a world? He wondered if Andrei Zakharchenko who dreamed of living in such a world found what he wanted by cracking his skull open with machine gun bullets.

Zakharchenko often came to Khanya in dreams. In the morning, after waking up Oleg could not get up for a long time. These dreams were very vivid and realistic as if everything was happening to him not in a dream but in reality.

Loneliness pushed Khanya out of the house, calling to the city streets. Anxiety ran under his heart in a catlike gait.

CHAPTER III

It was a dark spring night. A small room with posters of racing cars on the walls. On the floor there is a frying pan with cutlets. Next to it there is a bottle of vodka.
"I was miraculously not killed in that race."
Brushing his long, fair hair off his forehead with his hand, the fellow sits back in his chair.
"Give me a glass."
"Let's drink to luck!"
The glasses were empty. A hot wave of liquid enveloped his stomach. "I was lucky in my life, but I didn't know happiness," the fair-haired man belted out a song.
"Hey, Yura, I'll go. It's late."
Khanya, wobbling, got up. The fair-haired man weakly extended his hand.
"Bye... Why don't you stay?"
"It's time for bed. It's late."
"It's time," - Rakhit echoed, lying down on the couch.
"I'm off."
The fair-haired man nodded his head.
"Yura..."
Khanya stood at the door.
"What?"
"Keep in touch."
"Okay."
The evening coolness pleasantly refreshed his face. Oleg walked home leisurely. "Good guy, but he can't drink vodka," Khanya thought of the fair-haired man. - He's a genius at the wheel."
The air trembled strangely. The wind stopped. Oleg looked around in surprise. Listened. Looked at the clock. Half past one. Nothing unusual. A very typical spring night.

***

Time will pass, and hundreds of books will be written about it in different countries of the world. About how on April 26, 1986, at 01.24 Moscow time, an explosive wave knocked out the thousand-ton roof of the reactor at the Chernobyl nuclear power plant and split the building with a ginormous impact. The tragedy shook humanity, but not the Soviet government led by Gorbachev. The explosion, which caused the deaths of thousands of innocent people (not 31, as the official press claimed), in fact, was inevitable, for it was a link in the logical chain of the development of "developed" socialism. The only question was where and when it would happen, not whether it was possible or not.

The flame of the explosion, penetrating through the pores of human skin, illuminated people's souls. The world saw the true faces of the rulers of one-sixth of the earth's landmass. The policy of renewal, democracy, acceleration, and reforms gradually degenerated into fiction, leading to the crisis of the 1990s. It could not have been otherwise. The same blood flowed in Gorbachev's veins as in the veins of all the previous leaders of the Soviet Country.

Only on April 28, the USSR government timidly admitted the fact of the explosion. Children still played on the streets of Chernobyl, Pripyat, and Kiev, destined to die of diseases caused by the explosion. They would not be included in statistical reports because they did not die directly during the catastrophe. What would happen afterward was of no interest to anyone. At the time when in Bucharest the pro-communist regime of Nicolae Ceaușescu canceled May Day demonstrations, replacing them with indoor rallies, when in Western European countries, parents forbade children to play in the open air, in Kiev (the epicenter of the explosion was no more than 100 kilometers away) May Day was celebrated with special pomp. Who cares about the health of slaves? Here they march - happy, past the stands, waving flowers.

Let's show the whole world how easy it is to breathe! Why should someone care about the water, the food, and the soil poisoned with radiation? The slaves have work to do. In the name of the noble ideas of October. In the name of a bright future.

The scale of the tragedy became known a few days later, after the May Day holidays, when relatives of high-ranking officials left the dangerous city and the surrounding region. Kyiv residents experienced a true shock when they learned how severe the consequences of the accident could be. From several settlements located near Chernobyl, more than one hundred and sixty thousand people were resettled. After a while, it became clear that many had been relocated from less to more fallout-contaminated areas. Awareness of what was happening was virtually at zero. Dosimeters were chronically in short supply.

Moreover, the authorities took away existing dosimeters from the population and destroyed them, ostensibly to prevent panic. In reality, this action further increased the already depressed mood of the population. People realized only one thing: they had to run away. The faster, the better. Anywhere, as long as it was far away from Kiev. People rushed to train stations and airports. Ticket prices rose to astronomical heights. "Run away," was the only thought pounding in people's minds.

At certain time, the radiation situation was broadcast on the radio. People stopped on the streets, squeezed through the crowd closer to the radio, catching every word of the announcer.

A gaunt old man approached one of these crowds, stopped beside Khanya, and wiped his high forehead with a laundered handkerchief:

"I've seen this once before, son," – he said, either to Oleg or to someone else. – "During the war," – he said in a quiet, calm voice. – "Just like that, people gathered in the streets near radios. Standing silently. Waiting for good news."

***

The phone call unpleasantly grated on his ear, interrupting his sleep. Oleg fumbled for his slippers with his foot, moved the phone closer to the bed, and picked up the receiver.
"Are you asleep?"
A familiar voice came from far away, as if from the bottom of a well.
"I'm asleep. Alexei, is that you?"
Laughter in reply.
"Yes, it's me. Hello, Oleg!"
"I thought you've already forgotten me."
"It's not in my rules to forget good friends. What has exploded there?"
"A reactor at the nuclear station. You can't imagine what's going on here! People are living at the train stations just to get away."
"You're here, aren't you? Why didn't you leave?"
"I only got a ticket to Lviv for tomorrow. I couldn't get it earlier."
"Tear the ticket."
"What?"
"Listen to me. Don't go anywhere. My friends and I will come to your place soon. Got any money?"
"I don't know"- Oleg hesitated. – "A little bit."
"We'll bring the money. You say the people from Kiev are leaving?"
"Yeah, almost all of them."
"Great. Rent three or four apartments. Preferably, the apartments should be poorly furnished and more spacious. Get drivers for two cars and a truck. Don't spare any money. Promise a high salary. It'll all be paid for. We'll also need a big storage facility, bigger, more spacious and out of sight. A half-abandoned building would be ideal. Understand?"

Oleg did not have any idea. What drivers? Why apartments? What storage facility? One had to be an idiot to go from Leningrad to Kiev at this time.

"I don't understand."

"I'll explain when I arrive," the familiar voice interrupted rudely. - Did you understand everything?"

"Everything."

"Will you do it?" – There was a hint of doubt in his voice.

"Yeah. I'll try."

"Try," - in Alexey's voice, you could clearly hear the slyness. – "If you said yes, you must do it. You must be responsible for your words. If you do everything as I said, you'll earn good money. Wait."

Short beeps. Oleg hung up the phone. Thoughtfully looked at the phone. Went to the bathroom and put his head under the cold water. He did not understand anything.

***

Four days later, the doorbell rang.

"You don't look fresh. Did you remember to have breakfast? - Alexei said instead of greeting, rushing into the corridor accompanied by a gray-haired man and a young fellow. - Is everything done?"

"We have cars, drivers too. Renting apartments is hard. I rented only one apartment. But it's a three-room apartment with high ceilings and in the city's center."

Alexei smiled."Great! What did I say?" - he turned to his companions. – "Oleg is a reliable man. If he said he would do it, he will! Get ready Oleg! Your star time has come!"

And he laughed.

The gray-haired man rattled a kettle in the kitchen, although he was not invited to the apartment. A young guy hummed something nervously under his nose, unpacking a blue sports bag

***

Nothing unites people of different ages, faiths, life goals, and interests like money. Whatever it is, money is a symbol of prosperity and confidence in the future. In a way, money is freedom. It gives you a chance to live your life how you want, not to waste your life on earning crisp papers to spend the accumulated money during the lunch break between two halves of the working day.

Money itself can be neither good nor bad. The same bill can buy a murder weapon and medicine for a seriously ill person. The question is what exactly this or that person spends money on and how he or she treats it: as a goal or as a means to an end.

In the months following Alexei's arrival, Khanya met more people than he had ever encountered in his entire life. During this period, Gosha, Vladik with his street gang, the old woman Valya, and many others appeared in Khanya's life. Alexei, possessing a remarkable talent for leadership, was able to make all those who fell into his field of vision work for him with obvious benefits. Curiously enough, Alexei himself always remained in the shadows - outwardly, everything came from Khanya. Everyone wondered where Khanya got so much money, connections, opportunities, power.

Alexei's idea was extremely simple. I would say even primitive. Another thing is that no one else had thought of it in a similar scope at that time. The basic idea was to buy up everything that came to hand: imported furniture, equipment, carpets, antiques... absolutely everything! After the Chernobyl accident, panic reigned in Kiev. People were selling their property for next to nothing. They needed money. Many people thought that they would never return to Kiev.

The two-room apartment rented by Oleg was quickly filled with things. They had to look for a warehouse within the city. Despite the fact that they managed to ship only part of the goods to Russia, Alexei continued to invest.

"Oleg, look at things soberly, - argued Alexei once late at night, stirring sugar in a cup of coffee with a spoon. - Nobody is going to leave forever. People will run out of money and panic, too. Everyone will return to Kiev, even if the radiation is unusually high here. Some will die, and others will be born. They'll never leave Kiev. Besides, in fact, the country's entire population is under house arrest. Is it for nothing that Soviet citizens had registration at the place of residence? Without registration at the place of residence, you will not be hired, and you will not be given housing. Not everyone can steal. Therefore, whoever is registered will go back there. If we don't resell the goods in Russia, we'll sell them here to those we bought them from. How did Marx put it? Real money is money plus profit."

Alexei reveled in his own greatness.

Simultaneously with buying, selling, and reselling things, the gray-haired man and the young guy from Leningrad skillfully used the local thieves to burgle the apartments of citizens who left the city. In all the hustle and bustle, the police had no time to investigate burglaries, and if they did make a search, it seemed to have no effect.

***

When exactly the man with soft and tired voice had appeared, Khanya couldn't remember. Maybe the day Rakhit arrived from Pripyat?

"We hardly got away," - said Rakhit, sitting down in his chair.

"We didn't take anything in Pripyat. We couldn't even enter the city. There are police checkpoints on the roads everywhere," the gray-haired man said. – "We drove around the nearby churches."

There were icons and church books in the backpack.

"What's this?" – Alexei was surprised to see "Playboy" magazines in the backpack. They were neatly enclosed in a torn plastic bag.
"We took them with us so you and Khanya wouldn't be bored."
Everyone laughed except the guy in the chair. That's when Khanya first noticed him. Who is he? Where did he come from? Fair hair, short athletic haircut, blue eyes. His soft and tired voice expressed not so much his inner state as his attitude toward the world around him. It seemed that such a man could have neither enemies nor friends nor those whom he could love nor those he would hate. To everyone, to everything did he show an even, friendly attitude of a man spoiled by life and tired of it.

***

"Money not invested in business is dead," Alexei liked to say. - And so are people. As long as they are in motion, as long as they are running, as long as they are solving problems, doing something, even if it is not necessary for anyone, they have life in them. When a person stops, he will immediately find himself in a coffin under the ground. Life is movement."
Shortly before the New Year, Alexei, having explained to everyone what to do and having sent the cars to the city, stayed alone with Khanya.
"Oleg," - Alexei began ingratiatingly but rather stiffly, putting his feet on the kitchen table. – "Do you remember who you were six months ago?"
"Why do you ask, Alexei?"
"I wanted to remind you. People have bad memories. People who were beggars yesterday and now have hundreds of thousands are dangerous people. As a rule, they have short memories and short lives."
Oleg was tense and silent. Alexei continued:
"Why did you start earning so much? Because you carefully followed everything I told you. Isn't that right? That's right. If you

want to continue getting good money, then in the future you should not only do but you must do everything I deem necessary. I'm the boss. Do you agree?"

"Sure."

"Apparently, I'm not mistaken in you and not in vain I put you above everyone else, assigning myself the modest role of your senior friend, which has nothing to do with business." – Alexei smugly reveled in his own greatness. - "It is necessary that everyone considered you and only you the boss. Tomorrow night you will gather all of us. You will have to divide the bulk of the profit among them, and you will divide it. Mind you, some people may not be satisfied, but you don't have to worry about that."

***

"You promised everyone a fair share,"- Gosha jumped up with a glass of vodka in his hand, indignant.

"That's right,"- Khanya replied calmly. – "You'll all get your interest. Twenty-five percent will be left for the development of our business, and this money will be kept by me. The rest of the money will be divided equally - half for me, half for all of you."

"Do you know what they can do to you for such distribution of profits?" - The gray-haired man crossed his arms on his chest.

Alexei smirked wickedly:

"It's stupid to argue. Khanya is completely right. The idea is his, and the money, too. He brought us all together and let us work for a profit."

The gray-haired man glanced warily at the man with soft and tired voice who stood silently behind him.

"Khanya lives by the laws of thieves, and I agree to take my share."

The stack of money went into Alexei's hands.

***

The dead of night. The time is between three and four o'clock. The time when everyone sleeps - the contented and the cursed, the cowards shivering in fear, and the brave boasting about their strength.
Two shadows in the muted light of the desk lamp.
"All clear. Just like in a fairy tale, as you can see, all dreams come true," - Alexei gave Khanya a fatherly pat on the head. – "Where's the money?"
"Here."
Alexei put the money for business development and Oleg's money into a sports bag. The same bag he'd come to Oleg with the first time.
"This is yours." - Alexei threw the wad of money on the desk. – "It's only fair."
Alexei straightened up, glaring questioningly at Khanya with ant-like eyes as if waiting for a punch.
There was no emotion on Oleg's face.
"As you divided it, so be it. It was your business."
Oleg pressed his lips together dispassionately. The waves of the black hair fell on his forehead.

***

There were a lot of calls in the morning. After lunch, there was a ringing silence. Oleg lay on the sofa with his hands behind his head. His eyes tiredly studied the cracks in the ceiling. Laziness, emptiness. The state was like that of a sprinter when the finish line and the screams of fans in the stands were a thing of the past.
The doorbell rang. "I don't want to answer the door," Oleg didn't move. - I'm not home."
A rattle in the door lock. Someone was trying to pick a lock. A few minutes later, the door opened.

"Do you want your skull crushed, or do you want it crushed later?" - Khanya raised himself up on his elbow.
"Did you tell me everything?" - A soft and tired voice.
"Everything."
"You didn't thank me."
"For what?"
"At least for the fact that at least someone cares whether you're alive or maybe you're no longer alive," - there's no excitement or threat in his voice. Fair hair. Blue eyes. – "Alexei stitched you up. To everyone, he's innocent."
The man with the soft and tired voice carelessly ran his finger along the edge of the crystal vase.
"You are to deal with thieves about what was, what will be... Nobody needs competitors, and rich competitors in particular. Not to mention the ones who keep the gang together by pretending to be the leader. Besides, everyone knows you have a lot of money... Well, I don't think you do."
Pause.
"Sooner or later, you'll have to talk to the police, not Alexei."
"What do you want?" - Khanya interrupted.
"Me? I haven't figured it out yet. I get moral satisfaction from talking to you. Alexei is not a bad man. But he's a bit greedy. He showed everyone that the money is yours, not his. Why? Because Alexei couldn't have more than 200,000 after his wanderings. He, however, invested at least four million in the business. Mysterious. By the way, he shouldn't have killed Zosik. It was shortsighted and stupid."
"There's no blood on Alexei from that case."
"Don't be naive. Did you also believe in the masquerade with the rest of the money found?"
"Everyone believed it, but you didn't?"

"People believe what's good for them. Alexei's return to Leningrad as a man innocent in Zosik's death benefited many people. When there's a notion of profit, people turn a blind eye to many things."
"It's none of my business."
"You're wrong. That's what I'm here for. Alexei announced that he was going away for a long time and might even retire. That's not surprising, though. With such money, one can do charity work. No one knows about Alexei's future plans, but you must have bought the train tickets for him. I'm not asking where exactly he's going. I just want to know when and the number of the train."
"Why?"
"I want to say goodbye to an old friend."
"I didn't buy Alexei tickets."
The guest sighed and stood up. Taking hold of the handle of the front door he said,
"I feel sorry for you. You are more unlucky than I was."

***

The sun was approaching the roofs of the houses. Oleg lay on the sofa, staring at the ceiling. There was emptiness in the soul. Nothing but emptiness. No joy or sadness, only inexplicable indifference to everything surrounding him. It was not just the absence of feelings. It was as if everything was frozen inside and around - a boundless desert, life without taste, color, or smell...
The emptiness in the soul was like a long, empty corridor at the end of which there was no exit. Everything around seemed monotonous and endless. After the busy months, life returned to its usual rut, becoming a gray, monotonous sequence of days devoid of meaning. Khanya had no desire to do or feel anything. He didn't want to get up from the couch.
The phone call drowned out the sound of the TV. There was a familiar voice on the phone:
"Didn't I wake you up? No? Hello! Nothing is changed?"

After a moment's hesitation, Khanya got up from the couch.

"Changed." - In the telephone receiver he heard the creaking of wires, the footsteps of the crowd of passers-by. – "Alexei is leaving today. The twelfth carriage. The fifth seat."

On the TV screen, a flock of children were carrying armfuls of flowers to the foot of the monument to the founder of the world's first socialist state. Happy children. A well-fed life. Bright future.

CHAPTER IV

Ahmed had no reason to worry. Talks about the crisis awaiting the country in the near future and politicians' forecasts did not worry the gray-haired mountain- dweller. The introduction of Prohibition in 1985 and the anti-alcohol propaganda that followed it served as a powerful impetus for the development of the drug business. People started looking for an alternative way to relax, forget about problems, and escape from the realities of everyday life. The Law prohibited legal access to alcohol, which created a void and discontent among those who were used to drinking. In search of a substitute, many increasingly turned to drugs, which became available through illicit networks.

As a result, the demand for drugs increased significantly in Ukraine, and drug traffickers quickly found ways to meet this demand. Previously, until the mid-eighties of the last century, few people had heard of drugs in Ukraine.

Increased drug sales stimulated crime. Alcohol prohibition and the black market associated with it created the conditions under which drugs became a very lucrative business. No one cared about the health and well-being of ordinary people. Ahmed and others like him were interested in profit only.

The drug business brought Ahmed so much money and power that he could only dream of before. "The boys do not feel the lack of clients," - liked to repeat Ahmed, demonstratively shuffling in front of friends stacks of money. In Kiev, Ahmed felt at ease, not at all like in his native Caucasus, where he was perceived as a mediocre six in a deck of labeled playing cards.

***

Khanya woke up to a scream. Someone was shrieking, howling, mooing. Very loudly and somewhere very close by. The sound of shattered glass and the cracking of broken furniture added to the shrieking, "They're killing me". His gaze fell on the clock. Six twenty in the morning. Having put on his shirt, Khanya looked out the window. A stout man from the next doorway, in torn family underwear, barricaded himself on the balcony, desperately fending off the onslaught of the guys trying to extract him. The half-asleep occupants of the neighboring apartments watched curiously, commenting noisily on what was happening.

A police patrol drove up to the entrance. The noise in the apartment died down for a while, then erupted again. Everyone - attackers as well as defenders - were crammed into one car and driven away. Oleg expected to see among the attackers athletes with over-pumped muscles, but instead, they appeared to be skinny teenagers with frightened eyes.

"They should eat ice cream after school, not fight in the morning," - said the neighbor a floor above.

The phone rang loudly.

"Baranovsky's been arrested," Vladik said. – "Drugs and hookers. We should have him released."

"We're not his good service shop."

"They'll put him in jail."

"What's he being prosecuted for?"

"Misdemeanor disorderly conduct."

"The day started off badly," Oleg thought irritably, getting back under the warm blanket.

***

It was impossible to look at Baranovsky without laughing. It was the first time in his life that Vladimir had been detained by the police. His whole appearance spoke of deep remorse and plea for help and compassion. The expression on his face did not match the figure of a heavyweight boxer. Big, strong, and frightened. The contrast was so striking that even the investigator could not refrain from laughing.

For the first time Oleg saw Baranovsky near the gym where Vladik was improving his skills in sport during a break between boozes. Then, he saw his photo in the newspaper "Soviet Sport", somewhere on the last pages. Later, as a regular Vladik's companion. The passionate admirer of snow-white shirts always kept the boxer near him. Baranovsky was fine with that. "I am where the money is," he used to say with an arrogant smile. In fact, Vladik had money.

***

Faded curtains. Miserable furnishings. Expensive clothes. A dirty floor that had never been cleaned.

Vladik lay on the wide bed, indifferently watching a blue-eyed blonde with a slim waist kissing the toes on his right foot. He had called Khanya a few minutes before. That was the end of Vladik's worries about the boxer's fate. Khanya will help Baran out. He has money, connections. And if he doesn't - to hell with him, it won't be a problem to find another fool who spent half his life jumping in the boxing ring for the monthly wages of two janitors in a restroom. There are plenty of poor athletes out there. Khanya said it right: "Your business is to execute. My business is to think." Vladik rolled over on his stomach. He ordered:

"Give me a massage."
The woman's hands obediently began to rub his back.
"Like this. Lower," - Vladik yawned contentedly. – "What do you think I like most of all in women?"
The blonde laughed nervously:
"I don't know. Probably breasts?"
"Stupid, I don't mean the body."
"Not the body? Maybe fidelity, affection...."
The tip of her tongue touched the base of his spine. Vladik moaned with pleasure.
"Fidelity... Caress... Bullshit."
Vladik climbed out from under the blonde. Slapping his bare feet on the unwashed floor, he headed for the bathroom.
"So, what do you like the most?" - The blonde asked lazily.
To be fair, she wasn't stupid. Through the tobacco smoke that hung in a cloud from the ceiling, it came out:
"An animal. Sleeping in each of the women. Awakening on the eve of intercourse. An animal that is stronger than me but which I control. Because I am the man, and you are my animal. Just like everyone else."
The sound of the water in the bathroom drowned out his voice.

***

The police department. Portraits of Dzerzhinsky and Solomentsev over the desk. At the table opposite Khanya is an investigator. Khanya shrugged his shoulders feigning sincere remorse:
"What drugs? Drunk. He's remorseful... His whole life is in sports. Hitting on girls? He didn't maim or rape them. It's a shame about the fellow. We'll be grateful."

***

"Thank you, Oleg, I'll never forget," - the boxer mumbled ingratiatingly as he left the police station.

"I won't put your "Thank you" in my pocket."

"I'll work it off! Just tell me what to do! "

Not far from the entrance to the police station, four teenagers, head down, were listening to a solidly built man in his forties. "Where have I seen them?" - Khanya thought.

Suddenly it dawned on him. Early morning. The scream of a neighbor. The police. Six twenty in the morning. The man raised his eyes to Khanya. It was the strong look of a strong man.

***

"If you don't learn to work clean, you'll rot in jail till you're old. I'm not going to waste my time on solving your problems every time. Understand? Go home now. You'll come to me tonight. Maniunya!"

"I'm here, Ahmed."

"Who's that next to the boxer?"

"That's Khanya. He took advantage of the fact that during Chernobyl, all the respectable people left Kiev. They say some of the famous thieves supported him."

"Whoever supported him, we'll put anyone in their place. Do you understand me?"

"Yes."

"The police have a plan, too. They need to put someone in jail."

***

Khanya saw in the New Year in 1987 alone. Having announced to everyone that he was going to Moscow for the holidays, Oleg filled the refrigerator with food and enjoyed the peace. The hustle and bustle of the previous months had shaken his nervous system. He wanted silence and... reason. Exactly - reason. Communicating with Gosha, Vladik, and the like did not contribute to his intellectual growth. Rather, on the contrary. Oleg felt how much the past six months had changed his speech and, therefore, thoughts. It seemed that not on the books in the bookcase but on his thoughts was a dense layer of dust. Oleg leisurely ran his index finger along the spines of the books. How strange! Those who wrote these books many years ago control the thoughts and desires of those who live today and shape the future.

***

The man with a soft and tired voice appeared in the first days of January when everyone in the house was still asleep. He came into the room without undressing and dumped the money on the thick carpet:
"This is your security and, in a way, your future. Now you will be able to close all questions - both with thieves and with the police."
"What about Alexei?" - Oleg picked up one of the packs from the carpet.
"Forget about him or remember him with gratitude. You can't think badly of him now."
Khanya felt the clammy tentacles of fear gripping him.

***

Marina sprinted out of the Rus Hotel. The drunken foreigner, swaying from side to side, either hugged her around the waist or held on to her jacket. The girl turned her head away from his kiss with disgust.
"I have to go home."
"What home? What are you, a bitch? You're coming with me. I paid for you at the restaurant."
He slapped the girl's face with a relaxed palm. It wasn't hard, but it was painful. Tears sprang from the girl's almond-shaped eyes.
"Stop!"
The car slowed down. Rahit looked back.
"Did you forget someone?"
Khanya opened the door.
"Perhaps."

Gosha followed his gaze indifferently.

"The girl would deal with her boyfriend."

Khanya got out of the car. Gosha fidgeted nervously:

"Rahit, why did he go there?"

"Khanya is bored."

Rahit looked curiously through the tinted windows.

"Why are you hurting the girl?"

Behind the foreigner's back a broad-shouldered brunette with a shy smile.

"Mind your own business. I paid for her."

"How much?" - The brunet asked calmly.

"I don't feel sorry for the money."

In the brunet's open palm were five hundred rubles.

"Take it for her."

Drunken eyes stared at the bills. A short blow. The back of his head, with a red stripe, cut the ice under his feet. The foreigner's uncomprehending eyes swiveled from side to side. The money went back into his pocket.

"Get in the car!"

"I'm not a thing that is traded!" - Marina yanked her hand away.

"Rakhit!"

The car took off from the place. Several people of Caucasian nationality ran to the rescue of the fellow countryman. Marina barely had time to duck her head, thrown into the back seat. A rough hand grabbed Khanya by the shoulder. On a sweep, without looking, Oleg struck in the face of the attacker.

"Let's go!"

Jumped into the car. Someone tried to grab the BMW behind. Slipped and fell into the dirty snow. Rakhit drove the car confidently. On Victory Avenue, he slowed down.

"Where to?"

The girl turned away. Khanya leaned forward sharply.

"Turn around. Beauty dreams of going back to her friends."

"No," - the girl had a very beautiful, melodious voice. – "Take me home, please."
She had a pleading look in her eyes.
Rahit's questioning look. An affirmative nod of the head.
At the entrance of her house, the girl clapped her eyelashes warily:
"You have nothing to tell me?"
Oleg shrugged his shoulders:
"It seems not. Actually, I would like to be friends with you, but you're clearly not in the spirit. I'm not imposing myself."
"You're not imposing. See the balcony? Third floor. The twenty-seventh apartment. You can come in if you want. Thanks for helping me out."
She waved and disappeared down the stairs. Khanya returned to the car. Gosha was rummaging through the glove compartment, looking for matches.
"Tell me, Oleg, why do you need this girl and her problems?"

***

The year 1987 changed the consciousness of the Soviet people. Private companies began to be established practically throughout the country, thus striking a blow to the basis of Marxist-Leninist philosophy - the denial of private property. The dominant ideology, anticipating agony, blamed Brezhnev's ruling for everything, although, in fact, these were the most stable years in the life of the Soviet state. The media with increasing frequency published articles against Stalin. Ahead was the October Plenum of the Central Committee of the Communist Party of the Soviet Union, which would name the future president of Russia - Boris Yeltsin. However, this will be later.
On the calendar - the beginning of 1987. People's consciousness has not yet been awakened. The irreversible process of revaluation of values was just beginning. Salaries and incomes in private enterprises did not fit the notions of a Soviet person, who since

childhood had been accustomed to poverty and to the idea that rich entrepreneurs were to blame for all misfortunes because they cruelly exploited those who worked honestly for them. The police were not in a hurry to protect private entrepreneurs from criminals. In fact, private business was unprotected. The word " racket," which was unfamiliar until now, came into common speech. Besides, racket turned out to conceal big profits. In prisons, it was all they talked about. Naturally, no one was going to work. Not even for good money. Everyone wanted to make a profit, and in order to do that, it was necessary to unite in gangs. The gangs were well-organized and fundamentally differed from those that had been there before.

A gun and a knife are convincing arguments in skillful hands. But not enough. For serious cases, you need brains.

***

"How much is it?"

"Two hundred."

"Isn't that a lot?"

"It's not expensive. I used to sell these for 300. I kept one for myself."

"Then why are you selling it?"

"I need the money. Look, it's imported, France."

The cosmetic kit went into the down jacket pocket.

"Money?"

"Ask this guy.

Two tough fellows. Both are in tracksuits."

"Money?"

The buyer grabbed the makeup kit and disappeared into the crowd.

"What money? He's not with me."

He replied with a cackle. The saleswoman looked at him, confused.

"I gave you the kit. Where's my money?"

"Leave me alone, or you'll lose your health."
The fellow leisurely walked on. The place was very crowded with both buyers and sellers.

***

"Khanya, your order."
A devoutly sweet voice.
"How much is it?" - Khanya twirled the brightly colored box in his hands and tossed it carelessly into the pile.
The fellow's eyes went wide. Which was stronger, profit or fear? Fear was stronger.
"Three hundred... no, two hundred. She asked for three hundred. I paid two hundred."
"Take the money."
Crumpled bills between Khanya's fingers.
"Are you not lying?"
"I promise! Two hundred!"
A BMW with tinted windows drove away from the meeting place.
"Where are we going?" - Rahit asked.
"As I see it, Khanya wants to relax with someone," answered thoughtful Gosha."
"Do you remember the girl we met near the "Rus" Hotel?"
"Apartment twenty-seven?"

***

Marina didn't open the door right away. When she did, she didn't seem surprised except that she cast a wary glance at Gosha.
"I think you're at odds with law."
"What do you mean?" - Gosha did not understand.
Oleg laughed:
"You have a difficult childhood and criminal past written on your face."
"You are observant."

"Keep quiet, the child will wake up."

Marina was dressed in a light silk house robe. Long but translucent, worn over her naked body.

"Where is your third friend?"

"In the car. He likes cars more than women."

"I see. Come on, I'll introduce you to my son."

The baby was asleep in his crib with his head tilted to the side.

"Won't wake up?"

"I think not."

Oleg looked around the room. Cozy but poor.

"Let's go to the kitchen." suggested the woman.

"This is for you."

"For me? Thank you," - an invisible ray from within illuminated her face, filling the woman's voice with warmth.

Oleg smiled. He was satisfied.

"Would you like to have lunch?"

He didn't feel like refusing.

"I feel awkward regarding Rakhit," - Oleg told Gosha in a low voice so that Marina could not hear.

"Khanya, it's not been half an hour since he ate. Not hungry."

Kitchen table. Ham. Salad. Dry wine. Oleg looked into the refrigerator in surprise. Strange how quickly the woman had prepared a meal almost out of nothing - the fridge was actually empty.

They had a snack and a drink. They talked a little bit about everything and, in fact - about nothing. Gosha went outside to see how Rakhit was doing. Marina leaned over to Oleg. The cold gleam of almond-shaped eyes.

"You gave me a cosmetic kit. Can I do whatever I want with it?"

The girl's look confused the guy.

"Of course, it's yours."

Marina stood up and threw the kit out the window.

"Why?"

"Tell me, which of the sales women did you steal this thing from?"
Khanya flared up:
"Explain. I don't understand."
"There's nothing to understand. The cosmetics you gave me have been used for quite a while and not by a very tidy woman, I suppose."
A thick color flooded Oleg's face. Shame mixed with the sharp vinegar of anger.
"Do I look like a man capable of such a thing?"
Marina put her hands behind her head - just like her son sleeping in the crib.
"Oleg, I see you for the second time in my life."
Gosha came back.
"Rakhit is OK. Reading a newspaper," - Gosha noticed the tense expression of Khanya's face.
Marina smiled coldly.
Gosha:
"Is something wrong?"
Oleg stood up.
"Apparently, we have to go."
"I thought you were in no hurry," - said Marina coldly.
Oleg did not answer. Gosha nodded his chin toward the room:
"Whose portrait is there on the wall?"
"Mom," she answered in an even, calm voice. – "She died a year and a half ago. Everything I have is thanks to my mom."
"And your father?"
"I don't know what a father is. Neither does my son."
"What did mother die of?"
Oleg flinched at the tactless question of the Tall Shadow.
"Breast cancer."
"I see. Mine hanged herself,"
Marina shuddered instinctively and hooked her fingers into the back of the chair.

"How is it?"

"Just like that. Knew, bitch, that I'd kill her after I got out of prison. So, she decided to do it herself."

"To say so about your mother. How can you do that?"

"I can," Gosha said hoarsely. - Because of her, my whole life is at odds with law, as you say. I wish I'd been home when my mother mutilated my sister. Face in the mirror. My mother wanted my sister to call a stranger "Daddy." She knocked my sister's teeth out. Then she gave my sister to her drinking buddies. They raped her all night long."

"How is that possible?" - Marina did not take her eyes off the tall man.

"Why not?"

To Oleg:

"Shall we go?"

Khanya stood up. Marina:

"Gosha, leave me and Oleg alone."

"Whatever you say..."

The front door slammed in the hallway. Bottomless almond-shaped eyes.

"Oleg... Stay, you're not in a hurry."

The voice is polite but cold. The steady, assessing gaze of an experienced woman. Khanya looked at the bed, then shifted his gaze to the woman. There was a breath of pleasure in the woman's open eyes. A bed that could have been warmed by the warmth of bodies. The mute question in her eyes was, "What are you willing to do in return for deliverance from loneliness?"

"I'm in a hurry."

The girl was not surprised by the answer. Silently closed the door behind the guest.

The guys went outside. Oleg shook his head reproachfully:

"Gosha, is there anything sacred for you in the world,?"

"Sacred for the saints. We are not saints."

CHAPTER V

The man with the rough and tough voice was introduced to Khanya by a blue-eyed blond man with innocent, lamb-like eyes.
"He has some fine abilities,"- the soft and tired voice characterized the newcomer briefly.
The man of some fine abilities sank heavily to a table at the bar. The chair beneath him creaked.
"Where did you find him?" Khanya asked.
"You mean Slon? I met him by chance."
"Slons are kind,"- Gosha cut in. – "And this one was not born but spit out."
"He is kind,"- said the blue-eyed blond.

***

It is amazing how the events of the external world change the inner appearance. Quiet, infantile Slon made the criminal world pay attention at him by sending Red-haired Stasik and Mukha to the intensive care unit. Slon realized that the thieves' laws were invented not to establish justice and order among criminals but rather to recognize that the strong could rob the weak with impunity, and the weak should not resent the strong for this. Human psychology is very interestingly organized. When money is taken away from you because you sat the wrong way, looked the wrong way, or spat the wrong way, it is not offensive because it is a deserved punishment. The key is to make the victim feel guilty.
The first time Slon saw the blond man was when he came home earlier than usual. He was very angry when he saw the strange young man having sex with his sister's best girlfriend.
"It's none of your business,"- said his sister.
"Maybe,"- Slon replied, pulling out a weighty hammer from under the kitchen cabinet. – "But why on my sofa?"

During the fight, the table lamp, the sister's friend, and the television got the worst of it. A woman's shrieking interfered with a full-blown conversation.

"I'm gonna tear you to pieces!" - the blond said goodbye

"Bitch..." -whispered back Slon.

The next day, they met at the dog park near Petrovskaya Alley and quickly found a common language. As a result, the union in Kiev increased the number of robberies.

Thanks to the blue-eyed blond, the higher echelons of the criminal world became aware of Slon, where the man with the soft and tired voice was very well-oriented.

***

Ten years ago, at the end of the seventies, to be more precise, on June 15 and 22, 1978, the criminal investigation officers, together with the workers of the State Security Committee, detained a suspect in the theft of icons from the Kiev-Pechersk Lavra.

The theft was committed so audaciously that even the worldly-wise detectives were at a loss. One thing was clear: the thieves were recidivists with experience. Another thing was unclear - how they managed to break into the well-protected premises. An employee of the Lavra, who happened to be at the scene of the crime, claimed that he was knocked down by a blow to the head: "I don't remember what happened next.

They were looking for a woman if to take into consideration the force of the blows. They were looking for thieves specializing in the theft of antiques. They checked fences, restaurants and dens of thieves. No luck.

"Enemy intelligence."

"Religious fanatics."

Talking nonsense! The head of the investigation department of the police in Kiev dismissed the delusional versions:

"The icons will turn up. If one person did it - it would be difficult to find, and here a group worked - so someone will blab."

And that's what happened. Less than a month later, one of the criminals bragged about the theft in the presence of strangers. It was the one who came up with the theft, a seasoned repeat offender. He had already been in prison twice before. Finding the accomplice was easy. At his first interrogation, Tima said with disdain to the cops' faces:

"Do you want me to betray my best friend I was in prison with? That's not gonna happen!"

It was really easy to find out who Tima had been in prison before. It turned out to be Vanya, a well-known criminal (petty hooliganism and extortion). Vanya immediately told everything and soon the third participant of the robbery was detained - a frail boy of twelve with unnaturally huge blue eyes. He climbed through the window into the room, broke the head of a museum employee with a wooden bar, and took out the icons. He acted without fear and on his conscience. You bet! Respected people called him to the crime! They trust him! They won't give him away! How could he have known at the age of twelve that the experienced criminals he trusted would immediately betray him after his arrest?

Eventually, Tima and Vanya confessed to everything and told all details. After handing over the loot, they were sent to prison by court order. The twelve-year-old blond boy was more difficult. He stubbornly kept silent and, as he was not beaten, did not utter a word. Moreover, the whereabouts of the two most valuable icons remained unknown. Persuasion and appeal to conscience and duty toward the Motherland led to the fact that the boy said in a soft and tired voice one single phrase:

"Fuck you..."

The investigators' patience ran out. The boy was put on trial.

In the colony, the blue-eyed boy proved himself to have sadistic tendencies and a moody, phlegmatic character. Much later, in 1988, sitting in the hotel "Rus," he said to Khanya in a flurry of memories and drunk cognac: "You know, Oleg, it was the best time of my life. We escaped through the barbed wire and did whatever we wanted. Food stalls, kiosks, savings banks, passers-by - we robbed everyone. We lived where we wanted and how we wanted! Once in Zaporizhzhya, near the river, behind the Palace of Sports "Yunost," we caught a couple in love. We raped the girl and beat the guy. We took away their money. The next day, I went to the "Children's World" and spent all the money to buy toys - a whole mountain!"

The police caught the blue-eyed boy with those toys. By the time he was released, the blond had earned two more convictions and served a total of eight years in prison. "We were returned to the barracks, beaten, tried. Some were sentenced to one more year in prison, others were given ten years. In the end, nothing changed. What difference did it make in childhood whether the court would give five- or eight-year sentence? None of us thought about it then. At that age, it seems that there is infinity ahead and life will never end. As long as the educators did not clamp our fingers in the door".

In 1986, the blond returned to Kiev. His father, who was being treated at the time for alcoholism, was happy to start drinking again and soon died. At the time of his father's death, Blond was at a friend's apartment, affected by drugs and singing "...the army didn't notice the loss of a soldier" in a soft and tired voice.

***

The duo of Slon and Blond whose nickname was Lord because of the tattoo on the wrist of his left hand) was very profitable for Khanya. In fact, Khanya assigned them the role of a kind of police, who monitored the order in the gang and his personal bodyguards.

However, Oleg was not in a hurry to bring them closer to himself because he understood perfectly well that such a tame is unlikely to succeed.

***

Since 1988, the rotting of pro-communist regimes proliferated. Romania collapsed. Ceausescu and his wife were executed. The unwanted people were also quickly shot. Then, Romania abolished the death penalty. In case of a new coup (in the opposite direction), it would be more difficult to kill the current winners. The process of democratization was in full swing in the countries of "victorious socialism." Czechoslovakia became agitated, Hungarians fussed, Germans timidly talked about the necessity to get the Berlin Wall fallen down. Even Vietnam proclaimed the need for restructuring.

Everyone responded to the events in Romania - Fidel in Cuba with preventive shootings of potential opponents of the government. Gorbachev - another chatter. In North Korea, however, it was quiet because the inhabitants were not told unnecessary things. In this country everyone is "equally happy".

Foolish Soviet people again believed that tomorrow would be better than today, forgetting that the entire history of their state suggested just the opposite - yesterday, not tomorrow, is incomparably better than tomorrow. However, for some categories of the population, the life indeed became better. Entry and exit abroad became much easier. Traders and hookers poured into Poland, Yugoslavia, Hungary... Quite quickly, a bright layer of constantly traveling peddlers aged 22 to 35 stood out from the number of new "pilgrims." Khanya did not like them because of their smugly unctuous faces, neatly pressed white scarves, and impudent arrogance.

"If they want to ride, let them pay. Otherwise, we will not pity them."

On the streets of Kyiv, Vladik and a pack of little kids took control of the "white scarves" in the places where they sold their products. Slon and Lord, together with respectable people from Uzhgorod and Lvov, blocked the roads through Western Ukraine. Robbing the traders was not very difficult. "White scarves" were characterized by a patina of pseudo-intelligence, lousy knowledge of foreign languages, pronounced selfishness, and outright venality. It was true what Alexey once said: when you do not have a penny, you are ready for anything; when ten thousand are put in your pocket, you will start to think whether it is necessary to take risks. "White scarves" did not want to suffer harm for the sake of those whom they called friends yesterday. They had their own concept of friendship, characteristic of peddlers.

On the basis of constant profits, Slon and Lord, working in close cooperation with local thieves, had no problems in Western Ukraine. Problems arose in Kiev. Vladik's boys were constantly feuding with the Caucasians. Ahmed was not going to share markets and businesses with anyone. He stubbornly did not want to recognize Khanya: "If I want to, I'll crush him." He wanted to crush him long ago but could not. The feud between the two gangs was limited to minor skirmishes. Meanwhile, the inevitability of war between them took real shape. Besides, it was unclear who should finally collect money from hookers and pimps, whose income in currency had increased sharply, since not only vacuum cleaners and TV sets were shipped abroad, but people as well.

Kiev criminals, joining the gangs at their own risk, went to neighboring countries to get something from the rich foreign pie. Many criminals wanted to restore order and establish the most favorable for themselves rules of the game, but no one ever succeeded. At the end of the eighties, Ahmed or Khanya could really have done it if they had found a mutually acceptable compromise. However, no one was going to find a compromise. Each one considered himself stronger and smarter than others.

And the more money they had in their pockets, the more their egos grew. The confrontation between the gangs was growing.

***

"Karina..." – She heard Ahmed's voice on the phone. – "I'm about to see you tonight."
Something between a question and a statement.
"Bring a girlfriend - my brother came from the Caucasus."
Ahmed called all Caucasians his brothers. Including the ones he robbed, framed, or gave to the cops.
"All right, sweetheart. I'll see if I can find someone."
Throwing a terry towel with a view of the night sea at high tide over her shoulder, Karina headed for the bathroom.
A year ago, the life of a pretty girl who came to conquer the capital from a remote district center changed abruptly. It happened at the moment when all dreams and hopes seemed to collapse forever. Karina failed the first entrance exam to the institute and cried bitterly sitting on a bench in the park. The girl did not notice how a dark-blue Volvo stopped behind, and a minute later, a voice with a strong Caucasian accent asked her politely:
"Can I be of service to you?"
Instinctively, she replied:
"As you wish..."
She looked up. The first thing that caught her eye was an expensive ring on the ring finger of his right hand and the majestic posture of a gray-haired Ossetian. An imported sports suit.
Ahmed was only courteous and polite during the first two weeks until Karina came to live with him. Unnoticeably, he was transformed into a rude, despotic owner, treating the girl as an ordinary thing which you can play with tirelessly and which it is not a pity to spend money on.
Eight o'clock in the evening.

"We are punctual," - two rows of marvelously snow-white teeth gleamed in Karina's smile. – "Meet my friend. We were taking entrance exam together."

"It was so long ago," - the girl blushed and extended her hand for a kiss. – "Lali."

The girls sat down at the table. A fat waiter obligingly poured champagne.

"I haven't seen her before," Ahmed said casually, keeping his eyes on the brunette.

Karina easily put her wrist on the shoulder of the Ossetian.

"You haven't seen many of my friends."

"You have a strange name," - exhaled Ahmed.

Lali carefully fixed her hair.

"My father is Georgian, my mother is Ukrainian."

A light evening dress. The fabric was tight around her breasts. The greedy eyes of a gray-haired man.

"My mother says I was named after my father's mother, who died a long time ago."

"Your face is familiar to me. Have we ever met in the Caucasus?"

"I've never been there."

"How come you haven't been to the Caucasus?"

"As you can see, it is possible."

"We'll fill that gap. Shall we dance?"

As he passed Karina, he said:

"The guest shouldn't be bored."

The guest's name was Hasan.

***

It was fun. There was a lot of champagne. There was a lot of music. There were lots of flowers. At the end of the party, when Hassan asked, "Which one is mine?" Ahmed answered in front of her, in front of Karina: "The blonde is yours." Why didn't Karina dig her nails into Ahmed's eyes? Why, as if in a hypnotic dream, did she go to Hasan's apartment?

Hasan was asleep. With disgust, Karina removed his hairy hand from her chest and pushed herself back to the edge of the bed. How humiliating it was to feel like a thing! Resentment, unspoken anger, despair, and tears streamed down her cheeks and further down her defiled body, dripping onto the sheet.

***

The next day about lunchtime, Ahmed brought Karina's things. He dropped a single phrase: "You'll live here for the time being." He talked to Hasan about something in the kitchen having locked the door. Just as suddenly, he left without saying goodbye. Among the things he brought, there was no jewelry and imported clothes which Ahmed had given to her as gifts.

A few days later, Karina saw her jewelry on her former friend. According to Ahmed, the jewelry was his property, and he had every right to dispose of it as he saw fit. To give, take them back, or give again.

When they met, Lali, as if nothing had happened, hugged Karina. Kissed her.

"It's all so sudden; I can't come to my senses. You're not offended, are you?"

"Of course not. We are friends," - Karina smiled, overcoming the pain as if from squeezing cramp. With hatred, she thought: "You say you can't come to your senses? I'll help you. You'll get your just deserts. You and Ahmed..."

CHAPTER VI

"Oleg, what are we going to do?"

Not Khanya, Oleg. That didn't happen to Gosha very often. When had Gosha ever addressed Oleg that way? A tall shadow huddled in the corner of the room between the warm carpet and the bookcase.

"Were there a lot of them?"

"A lot, Oleg..."

Oleg looked out the open window. Saturday night. Spring of 1990. What Khanya tried to avoid or at least delay for an indefinite, valuable time happened. Ahmed was the first to declare war. One condition - either he was the master in Kiev or nobody. Vladik was kicked out of his office, a store on the left bank of the city was burned down, another store was taken under control by the competitors. Besides, they took away the goods that were in stock.

"Ahmed's looking for you."

"When did he set up the meeting?"

"In five days, the middleman will inform us about the time and place. Today, during the fight, you couldn't be found. Neither by us, nor by them. Everyone's sure you're away, not in Kiev."

Khanya was in the library that day. No one could imagine to look for him there. Criminals don't go to libraries. Unless they're in prison. Never when they are free.

For Khanya, the library was more than just a place to read books. It was his sanctuary, where he found answers to many of his questions and found inspiration for the path ahead. It was the one place where no one could think of looking for him.

Khanya sat at a wooden table surrounded by tall shelves of books. He read everything he could get his hands on, from classical literature to scientific works. Perhaps this was his way of filling in the gaps in his education. Unlike many of his peers, Khanya did not attend university.

In the library, Khanya immersed himself in the worlds of other times and cultures, comparing different points of view. He realized that the world was far richer and more diverse than one could imagine.

"You would have warned me that this would happen," it was Rahit who put in his two cents' worth into the conversation.

"Warned about what? It was bound to happen sooner or later," Khanya's tone was mocking and sneering.

Rahit shut up.

"What are we going to do?" The man in the gray sweater repeated uncertainly.

"Do what? Prepare for the meeting. We have a few days to prepare. We have time to think. Get everyone to gather at your apartment."

***

It was a completely pointless conversation. There was a lot of emotion and no result in the end. Watching the members of his gang, Khanya was once again convinced that his people had no brains. They couldn't think at all. What at first glance seemed to be boldness and courage, was, in fact, a display of stupidity and narrow-mindedness. Toward morning, they crashed the dark blue Volvo of one of Ahmed's men, then drank vodka and, like tired sheep, went to bed.

Khanya looked at them all with irritation. Ahmed was acting cautiously and purposefully. He must have enlisted the support of the police. Otherwise, the Caucasian would not have dared to act so openly and brazenly. The reaction of the police was quite understandable. It was much easier for them to deal with Ahmed than with a badly organized pack of bandits and ex-athletes.

Khanya realized that there would be no mass brawl or shootout. That would play against him. In the end, Ahmed's men would remain at large, and he and his boys would be arrested and put on trial. He had to think of something and strike first before Ahmed did.

***

Khanya felt that he could not solve the situation with Ahmed alone. So, he tried to call Lord in Lviv. There was no answer for a long time. Twice, they hung up the receiver. The drunken voice whispered that blue-eyed blondes were not brought to the city in the current quarter.
Where to look for him? In Mukachevo? In Chop? It's possible to find him, in principle. But how long will it take?
Yura Rakhit brought two tank fuel canisters.
"Let them stay at your place for a while. There's a shortage of fuel in the city."
Khanya nodded his head mechanically, thinking how else he could reach Lord.
"By the way, blue-eyed Blond called you," Yura said casually.
"When?"
"Today."
"He couldn't reach you. Lord said that your phone is always busy. He and Slon are in Kiev now."

***

Blond was late. Khanya chewed his mint nervously, glancing back and forth into the alley. The lovers, the lady with a dog...
"I'm sorry. Like you, I don't like to wait or be late."
A familiar figure sank down next to Oleg on the bench.
"Any news?" Khanya asked.
"No good news, too much bad news. It's your own fault that things have gotten this far. Ahmed prepared himself for the war. A lot of Ahmed's countrymen came from other cities and the Caucasus. No one's going to be nice to you."
"The police?"

"They're on Ahmed's side. You know Ahmed pays well, and the police are corrupt. No matter how it ends, it's your guilt."

"Isn't there anything we can do?"

"In principle, there is."

Lord shook his head uncertainly.

"Ahmed will not go to extremes. It's enough for him to humiliate you in public and then make you work for him. I don't count broken bones and broken noses. If he does that to our guys, it's only to emphasize whose city it is."

"Strangers will not rule Kiev," Khanya said angrily.

"Who knows," said Lord calmly. "Moscow is ruled. Animals have a different discipline than ours. Animals, of course, have not grown to civilized society, but with such brains, they are just right for massacres."

"And ours?"

"What about ours? You can see for yourself. Everyone for himself, of course, except when success is guaranteed without consequences."

Oleg rose:

"I will kill Ahmed."

Lord smiled:

"I agree. The problem must be solved drastically. Just don't dare to pit pack against pack. It won't end well for anyone."

Khanya boiled up:

"Did I say something funny?"

There wasn't a shadow of a smile on Blond's cold face.

"Khanya, personally, you can't even lift a finger. Ahmed's being watched, and you're under surveillance. You're both making a big profit, and where there's serious money, there are serious people."

Khanya thought about it:

"Killing Ahmed won't be easy."

"More like impossible. Not only professionals are needed here, not only rich rewards..."

"What else?"

"How should I put it? It requires creativity. Ahmed has to disappear without a trace, to dissolve. Do you understand me? He must disappear without noise, without blood, so that no one can understand to the end what happened to him. You need smart people who will keep quiet and who you can rely on."

After a pause. Khanya:

"Do you know people like that?"

"There were a lot of people in prison with me, and murderers too. I've met a lot of them. I'll tell you what: every other person is capable of killing without thinking it through, calculating, weighing every little detail. To do it smoothly, without leaving a trace... Being silent as a gravestone... No, I don't think I know anyone like that."

"What's your advice?"

"If I didn't know the situation, I'd say do it all by yourself, alone, and then forget it, erase it from your memory. That's the hardest thing to do. It's not for nothing they say life is given by God, and only God has the right to take our lives. You don't just break the commandment "Thou shalt not kill." You are responsible for those who help you."

"Not everyone is a Christian."

"That doesn't make it any easier. Do you know what it feels like to kill another person? Standing face to face, not like in war, sitting a mile away from each other in your own foxhole? Seeing the life draining out of a healthy, strong body... Do you know what kind of dreams you may have afterward?"

"I've heard these stories told differently."

"Stories? They don't know anything about what it means to kill. If anyone claims it's easy to take another man's life, they're either a complete moron or a blabbermouth. You can't deal with them, no matter how sweet they seem."

The wind blew a chill in his face. The shadows of frightened birds flashed between the leaves. Khanya raised his head. He looked into the blue eyes:
"Can you personally help me?"
"I don't know," Blond smiled a strange, sad smile. "Ahmed knows how to make enemies. You are not the first. I've been approached with such a request before. It all seemed so simple. Ahmed's life was laid out in minute details."
"Why?"
"Why what?"
"Why did you refuse?"
"Kill the beast? I wasn't sure about the client; the one who asked to kill Ahmed was too emotional and psychologically unstable…"
"Who was it? Do I know?"
"Maybe you do. I'll think about it, Khanya."

***

Long beeps, and then:
"Yes…"
There's a soft, smooth voice on the phone:
"Good morning. Haven't waken you up?"
"Who do you want?"
"You. Hello, Carina."
"Who are you?"
"You used to recognize me right away. Have you forgotten how you offered yourself when you knew you wouldn't have enough money to pay?"
Silence.
"Do you recognize me now?"
"Yes."
"I need to see you."
"I understand. When?"
"Uh, now. I'm standing outside your house."

"Hasan will be back any minute."
"He's at the farmer's market. He won't be back soon. Spinning thimbles."
"Okay, I'll be right out."

***

They could have made a handsome couple. A tall guy with huge blue eyes and a bright girl who walked with him with a teasing, artistic gait. They walked side by side as if they were made for each other, their looks and style epitomizing harmony and beauty. The guy, tall and slender, had blue eyes that seemed as deep as the ocean. His hair was dark brown, and every step he took was confident and graceful. The girl walking next to him was a real beauty with long, thick hair that sparkled like honey in the sunlight. Her bright red dress emphasized her bright character and passion for life.

An elderly man with a shopping bag, who happened to be walking towards the couple, involuntarily slowed down and stopped for a moment, admiring the youth and beauty in front of him. His gray hair and wrinkles on his face were a testament to a long life full of joys and disasters. Nostalgia pierced his heart, and he remembered the bygone years when he himself was so young and enthusiastic. It was as if he had looked into his own past. Memories flashed vividly before the old man's eyes.

Unexpectedly for himself, the old man said in a low voice: "Be happy, children."

The boy and girl heard and turned around. They smiled at the elderly man and replied almost simultaneously: "Thank you!" Their smiles were sincere, and at that moment, it seemed that they were really happy.

Then they continued on their way, and the elderly man remained standing on the sidewalk and smiling. He felt warm and thought that even in this world of endless change and bustle, there was room for happiness.

***

Cigarette butts scattered across the carpet. The ashtray rolled under the table.
"I don't understand how you're going to get into Ahmed's apartment."
Khanya bent down to pick up the ashtray. He was nervous.
Blond laughed in a soft, tired voice:
"I won't just walk in. Me and Slon will be welcomed as the dearest guests."
Slon was sullenly silent.
"Who's driving?"
"You don't need to know. A nice guy from Ivano-Frankivsk."
Lord cast a quick glance at his watch:
- I don't like to be rushed. Did you get everything?
Slon nodded and, turning to Khanya, said:
"By the way, no one will know about this but us?"
"You could have not asked."
"I'm not asking. I'm reminding you."
There was a quiet click of the door lock. Khanya sank down tiredly at his desk. Rahit would pick him up in forty minutes, and they would go together to meet Ahmed.

***

Those who think that the politics of the state does not intersect with the politics of the shadow layers of society are mistaken. Minor politics logically reflects everything that happens in the higher echelons of legal power, like a mirror in a laughing room, where every little thing takes grotesque, ugly forms.
The life of thieves, sung in hundreds of street songs, lavished with a halo of romance, is, in fact, one of the most crude, primitive, and

dirty forms of human existence. Here, there can be no true friendship or pure love; everything is sold and shared - women, money, everyday objects .... everything is subordinated to one single goal - to live and get maximum physical pleasure at the expense of others. With no regard for kinship or any other ties. The transfer of money from one person to another takes place according to the simplest formula, primitive to the point of idiocy and contradicting the essence of big business, when the receipt of profit by one party satisfies the interests of other parties at the expense of which the profit itself is formed. There is no such thing as criminal life. There are always predators and victims on whose side the law and, in general, the whole state machine acts. Due to the presence of victims, the state regularly removes tribute from citizens in the name of the law, which means that criminals themselves provoke the state to increase the influence of those forces that are obliged to destroy them (those who have broken the line). Ultimately, the activity of criminals is aimed at their self-destruction. Due to the lack of intellect, and in general, constricted outlook, few people in this environment realize this fact. Those few who are able to think at least sometimes will keep silent because no one will allow them to take a swing at the structure of thieves' life, which has been created for decades. And in the former Soviet Union, this structure was created not so much by thieves as by representatives of the authorities.

All the talk about antagonism between the police (as well as prosecutors and other authorities) and criminals (thieves, crooks, and the like) is just insignificant. Criminals exist thanks to the patronage of police officers; police officers get rich thanks to criminals. This is an axiom that does not require proof because it is confirmed daily in real life. Those who have internalized it will have a chance to stay free longer than others.

Only teenagers and shortsighted people who have never been in prison think that criminals are inherently courageous, brave, generous, and the like. It's all nonsense. Daring deeds are most often dictated by the primitivism of thinking, when the way to get out of a situation is sought not through sober calculation or self-analysis but with the help of purely animal instinct, acting "on chance," often under the influence of alcohol or drugs. Moreover, those who have already served their time in prison are in real life more cowardly and meaner than those who have not yet been in prison. Because ex-prisoners know what they are risking and how it can end. That's why they put inexperienced young people in most risky areas.

Women like to have a lot of money spent on them. Even if there are no feelings at all. Criminals in expensive restaurants do not spare the loot, but it can hardly be called "generosity" - looting other people's money. Who doubts - let them see how yesterday's loved ones are 'sent to the brothel' ("I fed and clothed you - now work it off") or how profits are shared after a more or less successful robbery.

The life in criminal world is like a giant garbage dump where black-marked rats swarm in search of profit. They are called, like in a game of cards, the black suit. The few who manage to get out of this dump will never be able to completely sever all the threads that bind them to it. Even if they have intelligence and talent. Because the dirt you come in contact with is not the kind of dirt that can be washed off under a hot shower, having previously smeared yourself with imported soap. This dirt is absorbed not just under the skin and in the blood; it is absorbed into the structure of thoughts, it merges with the flow of feelings, and changes the luster of the eyes.

Observing the criminal environment, one is involuntarily inclined to think that it is not the hardened criminals that are much more dangerous to the authorities but the new formation which began to evolve in the mid-eighties and previously had no contact with the criminal world. Unlike criminals of the old formation who think in a standardized way with the same concepts developed by them, and not without the help of the police, this category of people is unpredictable in many respects. It is far from always possible to predict their actions and prove their guilt.

People like Khanya did not squander their talents on wallets with chewed three-rouble notes mixed with trolley bus tickets. They were cramped in a standard criminal environment. These people needed space. Big money was their lot. One shot to secure themselves for life. "Win it all or lose it all" is their motto, where "everything" really includes everything, including life.

They do not know how to be impertinent as scumbag criminals (deservedly or without reason brandishing a shiv under the very nose of the interlocutor), but their silence is worth paying attention to. They do not occupy prominent places on the rungs of the hierarchical ladder of the criminal world and do not become code-bound criminals, but they are smarter and, therefore, more dangerous. That is why they will always be reckoned with.

PART III

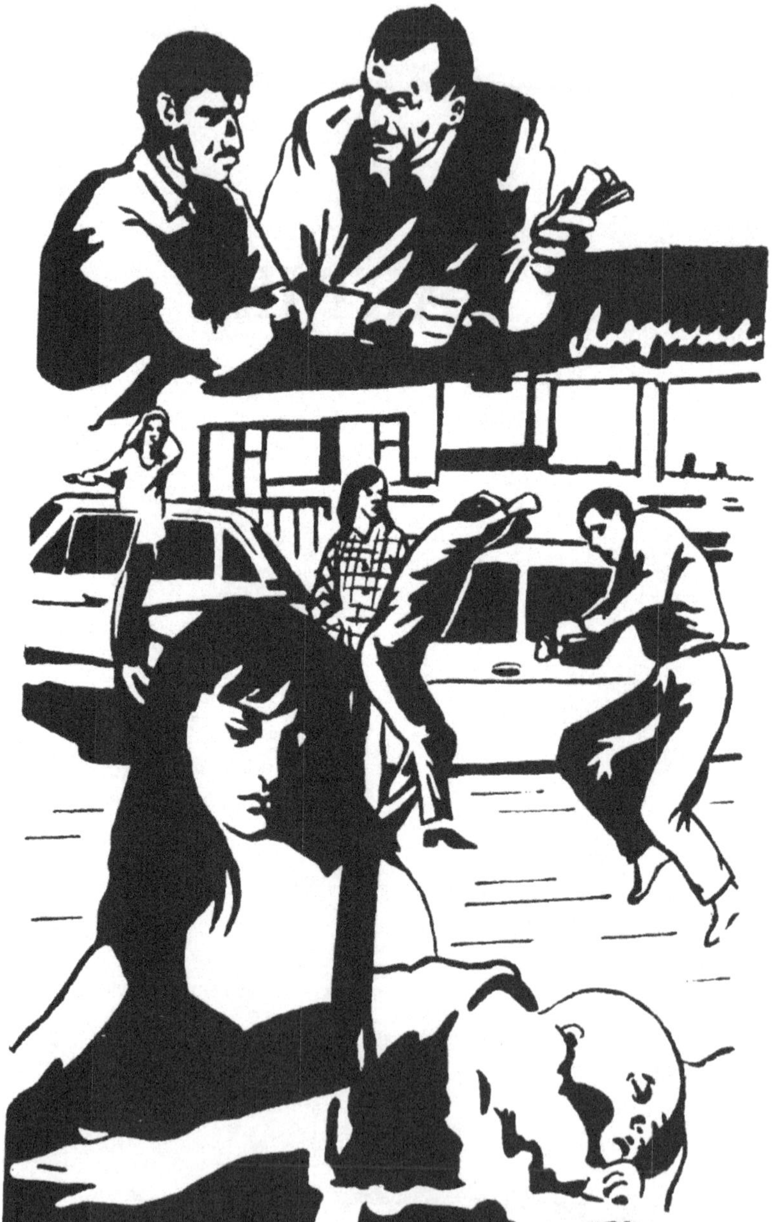

CHAPTER I

The traffic on the street was blocked by the police. Through the windshield of his BMW, Khanya silently watched the excited crowd hooting and hollering as the yellow and blue flag was raised over the city's main street. Most of those present were unkempt and drunk.

It seemed as if the whole world was now centered exclusively around this event. The noise and clamor of the crowd filled the air. Khanya and Rahit watched silently as the yellow and blue strip of cloth fluttered in the wind.

"Oleg, look - the crowd is hanging a rag instead of a flag."

Rakhit broke the silence.

"It's not a rag. It's the new flag of Ukraine."

"What was wrong with the old flag?"

Khanya shrugged his shoulders.

"How should I know? The old flag is a relic of the past, and the new one reflects the dreams of the Ukrainian people for a bright future. That's what they say."

"It's all nonsense. There is no future for these people. Look at their faces," Rakhit smirked, leaning back in his seat.

"Shut up," Khanya interrupted the driver gently.

Lately, he almost always said that when he was thinking hard about something.

Representatives of various street gangs, holding steaming coffee cups in their hands, came curiously out of the Khreshchatyk café. In fact, all of them, including Khanya, didn't care whether the mayor's office changed its flag or not, just like most Kiev citizens.

"I don't see any locals," Rakhit concluded casually, glancing through the crowd. – "All the people in the crowd are from Western Ukraine."

Khanya remained silent. What to say if everything was already obvious?

"Oleg Nikolayevich, my respect!" Semyon Davydovich came out of nowhere, standing near the car in a respectful pose. The lesson he learnt from Gosha and Korotyshka had obviously done him good.

"How do you like this patriotic act?"

Khanya grudgingly shook the sticky hand extended through the window.

"I don't care."

"That's what I'm saying. Nothing has changed ... What are they calling for?"

Semyon Davydovich listened.

"No, Kiev will never rise to the barricades because it has always been home to many business people who felt well under any regime."

***

Gosha was not interested in politics at all. He was indifferent to what was going on near City Hall.

"It would be better to do something useful." He said looking at the people hoisting a new flag over the central street of the capital of Ukraine.

Rejoicing like a child, he ran around the brand-new Volga. Vladik did not suppose that Gosha could be so happy about buying a car. Last year, after being cured of chronic gonorrhea, which was rather difficult, he felt much less happy.

Gosha drove much worse than Rahit, yet he was an aggressive driver, never gave way and disregarded safety rules. His new car became a weapon which he used to react vindictively to any unacceptable maneuver of other drivers. Gosha did not respect the rules and other road users, seeing them only as obstacles on his way to the pleasure of driving.

"It took me two days to get the papers drawn up," Gosha rambled, sitting down at the steering wheel."

"It's still nothing," - lazily waved his hand Vladik, who helped Gosha to register the car. Usually, the car registration process used to take more than a week.

Rumbling, Volga rolled out of the garage.

"It's all right. You can drive safely. Just don't speed up - repairs are expensive these days."

Vladik wiped his palms with an oily rag.

"Do you know the rules?"

Gosha laughed:

"You've never learned them either."

"It's up to you."

"Want a ride?"

"Me? Thanks. No need," Vladik looked at Gosha in surprise. Nodded toward Zhiguli:

"I'll get there myself somehow."

Volga rolled leisurely out of the gate.

The car changed Gosha's character. To everybody's surprise, he became very punctual and pedantic. Gosha stopped being late for meetings to impress the other members of the gang, but his egoism and self-conceit began to irritate those around him more and more.

***

Bright lights.

The door of a video salon is open.

Inside the room, on a large monitor screen, a Maltese dog jumped on the table, leisurely eating cakes while the hostess and the guest were talking in the bedroom.

The room is full of viewers. The air is soaked with sweat. A woman's envious sigh. The middle of a video session.

In a cramped room next to the auditorium, the owner of the video salon named Kudryavy is drinking martinis with a buddy who has come to visit him.

Since Khanya took control of the video salon, business has been booming. Although at first, it was a shame to share the profit with Khanya's gang. Kudriavy didn't want to pay security money to someone else and lose some of the profits. But he soon came to terms with the fact that Khanya took over part of the business. Especially since Kudryavy, with Khanya's help, had gained control of several more video salons.

Khanya not just took the money, he invested it in the development of the business as well. He got Kudryavy to renovate video salons, to make them look modern and cozy. Minimalist designs, comfortable chairs, and stylish lighting merged into a whole, and the interior of private cinemas was immediately updated.

However, the changes were not limited to the interior. Khanya proposed a new format for movie screenings: themed evenings, meetings with directors, and independent film festivals. This made it possible to attract a diverse audience and make video salons a place where one could not only watch films but also discuss them, participate in cultural events, and expand the circle of socialization. Later, all these video salons turned into very popular and full-fledged private movie theaters.

Khanya sought to make the business profitable and turn video salons into centers of cultural life, where people could enjoy the art of cinema and each other's company. Obviously, he already understood the need to legalize money and was preparing the ground for reorientation to legal business.

Every day, the number of visitors to Kudryavy's video salons grew, and profits increased. Porn movies, action, and horror films brought in the most money. These were closed sessions for a limited circle of viewers who were willing to pay good money to watch pirated copies of illegally imported videotapes from abroad. Things were going as well as they could.

Having waited until they were alone, the guy leaned over to Kudryavy:

"I need to talk to you."

Having nosed out profit, Kudryavy got excited. He had known the guy for years, heard he was a banker and made a lot of money.

"You have acquaintances, contacts among criminals. If you help me, I'll pay you well. I'm not greedy."

"Of course. I'll help you. I'm acquainted with serious people."

Kudryavy fidgeted impatiently in the leather chair. The guy licked his fat lips:

"A businessman is bothering my life. I need to get him killed."

The guy gave twenty thousand to the direct executors. Kudryavy, as an intermediary, would get five.

For a modern reader, such a fee for murder may seem ridiculous (what can one buy for such money?). However, in the summer of 1990, one could buy two new cars for twenty-five thousand rubles. By those standards, it was a lot of money.

***

It was no secret in the city who had helped Ahmed disappear. Going to Khanya, Kudryavyi was sure that his proposal would interest his host.

Khanya welcomed the guest in one of Kiev's bars. He listened attentively to the guest. He shook his head strangely, with a tinge of sadness. He asked again:

"Do you own a funeral parlour?"

The city noise outside the window and the clinking of dishes in the bar seemed distant and unreal.

"No."

"Neither do I. I wouldn't advise you to do that. Do you show movies in video stores? Then go on doing it."

He felt the disappointment slowly wash over him. The bitter taste of defeated hopes remained on his tongue. He had not expected such an answer.

It seemed that the conversation was over. But Kudryavy had already taken bail for the murder, and he didn't want to return the seven thousand.

***

A few days later, the guy came to Kudryavy's video salon.
"Any news on my issue?" He exhaled with the odor of badly chewed fish.
"'Yes, everything's fine," Kudryavy patronizingly patted his buddy on the shoulder.
"There are people..."
After a pause
"Serious people."
"Really?"
The guy's eyes lit up with hope and gratitude.
"You can rest assured."
Kudryavy decided to organize everything himself without Khanya. He didn't need money, but he was very greedy and thought that money was never scarce.
The night before, Kudryavy had talked to one of his regular customers, an ex-con who had served several years in prison for robbery.
He was an unshaven man with running eyes and large facial features. Thick black eyebrows, like clouds looming over him, gave the impression of restlessness and aggression. His large facial features made his expression heavy and gloomy. He was dressed simply but not without style. Black leather jackets and faded jeans were this man's everyday look. His shoes were heavy and sturdy, ready to run at a moment's notice. Several expensive but stolen gold rings shone on his fingers, like small trophies from the past.
He listened to Kudryavy carefully and immediately agreed.
"Money first."

Kudryavy grimaced.

"Better later. What if it doesn't work out?" Kudryavy argued cautiously.

"I won't make it? Either the money first or no deal. Besides, I'd have to leave town right away. We shouldn't see each other for six months after all this. For your own good. We aren't going to give the police something to talk about. Money first!"

That sounded convincing and logical. Kudryavy took the money from his buddy and the next morning handed it over to the hired killer.

***

The evening was so hot that the air seemed thick and still.

A light breeze from some unknown source tried to lighten the atmosphere a little, but it didn't bring much relief.

The hired killer leaned sleepily over an open can of sprat. His drinking companion casually flicked a fork off the table with his sleeve. The fork clattered against the empty bottles under the table and rolled under the TV.

His hand rose uncertainly to his mouth, and his fingers held the cigarette burning brightly in the gloom of the evening. In vain, he tried to shake off the mental pressure of this hot night and the cold flame of the cigarette.

"You've been given money."

His companion said.

"Not me, us!" Growled the big man.

"Yes. We've been given the money, and we have the money."

"We have a job to do."

"We have to, but on the other hand, it's dangerous to kill. You don't know how it's supposed to turn out."

"Yeah." They drank their vodka-filled glasses thoughtfully.

"Kudryavy's not a bad man. I don't want to let him down."

"Why let him down?" The drinking buddy got lively.

"Let's talk to the future victim. His task is to disappear so that not to interfere with other people's lives. Let him go somewhere far away for long, so that in Kiev they are sure that he is dead. He should pay us back for not killing him."

"That's an idea!"

"We won't have to kill anyone, and we'll split the money between us and save a man's life."

One last puff, one last crumbling white cigarette butt, and the drunken man threw his head back, releasing a cloud of smoke into the cracked ceiling.

***

The potential victim listened without fear to the threats of the unkemptly dressed men who came to his office during the working day. The bank director, a tall man in a strict business suit, nodded and made it clear that he was fully aware of what they would do to him in case of refusal. As a former state security officer, it was easy for him to throw out uninvited visitors. However, he decided otherwise:

"How much did they pay you for me?"

"None of your business," growled the big man, feeling the initiative slipping from his hands.

"That's right," the potential victim smiled.

"It's your business, but it's also my business. I'll give you exactly twice as much for directly bringing the man who hired you to me. So, how much?"

"Forty," the big man yelled out.

"All right. I'll pay you eighty. The money's in the safe."

There was a safe in the far corner of the room.

"You'll get the money right away. Just keep in mind I don't need any middlemen. I pay for the person who ordered me, not the person who brokered it. I want the name of the man who ordered my death."

The dumbfounded visitors came to their senses when the front door slammed behind them, and the fresh air slightly refreshed the gray matter called the brain in everyday life.
"Businessman. For that kind of money will I kill not only Kudryavy, but all his employees in the office."
"We need to find a contact before this businessman changes his mind."

***

The deputy director, pale, looked at the head of the bank.
"Will you pay them the amount of money?"
"Those fuckers? I feel underestimated. Within thirty seconds, they'll lose the will to live."
"Then why did you let them go?"
"Experience tells me they didn't come on their own. They were sent. By who? I want the name of the man who ordered them to kill me. We're going to have a special talk with that man. Did you really believe I was going to pay?"
"You spoke so confidently about the safe."
"There's not a cent in the safe. In the safe there are old company contracts of no commercial value. It's just paper. Go back to your workplace and do your job in peace. I'll take appropriate steps."
Having taken the folders from the table, the deputy director headed for the door. Behind him he heard the boss's voice on the phone: "...no...nothing special...just in case...three or four people will be enough for safety..."
Stepping out into the hallway, the deputy director felt his heart pounding frantically. "There's no way the boss will forgive me if he finds out. Kudryavy is not the man who will keep quiet, and he must keep quiet. So, there's only one way out. Only one."

***

Kudryavy stood with his head tilted to the side. Depressed, like an animal hunted by hounds from different directions.

"I told you it was none of your business. You didn't listen," Khanya said calmly and quietly."

"Take everything I have."

"I'll take as much as I need. That's not the point. You didn't listen to me."

"I'll do whatever you say."

***

It's half past three on the clock.

"Where's Gosha?" Khanya was furious.

"He's probably working on the car," Baranovsky said cautiously.

"After he had bought Volga, he was overly punctual at first, but then he became the same. He's always late," Vladik said with a cocky snicker. "Maybe we should burn his car to penalize him?"

Khanya didn't answer. They were extremely late for the meeting with the customer of the failed murder.

"There's no time to wait. We go without him."

***

A nod of the head instead of a greeting. A smooth-shaven face. Squinted eyes.

"Where's the guarantee that Kudryavy won't talk?"

"There's no guarantee. You have my word."

The deputy director smiled a troubled, short grin.

"It's not enough."

"You cannot choose."

That same evening, Khanya was paid twenty-five thousand. It was the video salon owner's silence money.

***

Gosha eyed Khanya warily.

"We got stuck on the road. If it hadn't been for Rakhit, I would have spent the night on the highway. I'm sorry I didn't arrive on time."

With a wave of his hand, Khanya interrupted Gosha's excuses.

"We'll talk afterward. We have a noble deed to do. How should we deal with those who not only took money for the work not done but also put friends at risk?"

"Take the money back. Beat them up so they don't do it again. Plus a fine," Korotyshka snorted obligingly. Khanya sarcastically patted the guy's cheek with the thumb and forefinger of his right hand.

"Good boy. Turns out you're not as dumb as I thought."

***

The hospital nurse on duty had completed her routine rounds of patients. She looked through the card with her notes and a list of urgent tasks for the night and breathed a sigh of relief, feeling the fatigue that had accumulated over the long day's work. It was late, and the moon obscured the light of the street lamps outside, creating a soft twilight. The woman made her way to the resident's room, where she could get some rest. She knew the night could be challenging, and she had to be ready for anything. Opening the door of the resident's room, she lay on the couch and closed her eyes.

The soft surface of the couch seemed like an oasis of paradise after a long shift. The woman tried to remain alert, but fatigue slowly began to pile up on her like an invisible weight. She knew she should stay on guard, but her body and mind demanded rest.

The quiet murmur of hospital sounds echoed in her ears: humming of medical instruments, monotonous noise of the air conditioner, and whispering of nurses at the station. The woman closed her eyes, her body in need of proper rest.

Time seemed to stretch on forever, and the woman fought herself to stay awake. She remembered all her patients who depended on her and her responsibility to them.

Her eyelashes fluttered. Beyond her will, the woman drifted into sleep. Somewhere in the distance floated the glare of the lamps in the operating room. The contours of patients. Snow-white sheets. A child crying. Her dream sucked the images of her brain into a mire of serenity, laziness, and peace. Deeper and deeper. The sound of the surf. A growing rumble. A construction site. Workers cursing. Dump truck. Broken rocks. Blood. Where'd the blood come from?

The nurse jumped up. Fixed her hair. A quick glance at the alarm clock face. Footsteps in the hallway. Someone is walking down the hall. Who could it be? All the patients were forbidden to get out of bed.

The corridor was empty, but the door to the corridor, which was always locked, was ajar for some reason. A hoarse wheeze echoed with the creak of the door hinges. Blind fear made the woman recoil. Curiosity pushed her forward. The woman peered timidly behind the door. On the floor, at the threshold, she saw the mutilated bodies of strange men. Their hands had been severed, and their tongues cut off.

***

Entry in the notebook: "Income. Received: from Kudryavy (fine) - 20,000 rubles; from the "Customer" - 25,000 rubles (help in solving a personal problem); from the executors hired by the customer - 15,750 rubles (the balance of the 20,000 given to them as an advance payment)." A little lower: "Total amount: 60,750 rubles. Expenses: Transportation - 400 rubles, to people for

"work" done - 15,000 rubles, lunch in a restaurant - 3,700 rubles. Net profit = 41,650 rubles."
Rakhit rubbed his hands together contentedly:
"Forty grand profit in a few days. Easy money!"
Half-lying on the thick carpet by the bookcase, Khanya languidly leafed through a seventeenth-century Bible in a gilded binding. Carefully, he blew away the dust that had settled between the pages. Raised his eyes to Rahit:
"Was that easy?"

***

There are "water-people" and "crystal-people." Humanity is like a river. Soft, pliable water only turns into sharp, unruly blocks of ice when at least one crystal falls into it. A few days pass and a large expanse of land is covered in ice. And so are the people. Look closely at a crowd of people. Like a stream of water, the crowd spreads out over the muddy streets. Hundreds of colors eventually form the gray color. The teeming crowd turns into a powerful, purposeful stream only when "people-crystals" get into it. I wonder if anyone, leafing through the pages of history, has ever thought about why some people were called "red" and others "white"? This is just a color, a suit of large crystals.

In the summer of 1990, Khanya set out to unite the power, influence, and money of separate gangs under his leadership. He was sure of success.

CHAPTER II

The evening was mild and warm, and the city life was pulsating. The streetlights came alive as night fell, and people began to come out of their homes to enjoy the night's entertainment. Vladik was going to a restaurant to relax. His psycho-physiological relief consisted of alcohol and new girls to help him fight boredom. In his regular, starched and pressed snow-white shirt, Vladik easily ran up the stairs to the hall. He slapped the waiter's ass unceremoniously (as a sign of deep sympathy and a kind of greeting) and headed to the table he had booked the day before, clumsily maneuvering between the dancers. Soft lights, soft music, and aromas of dishes created an atmosphere of coziness and romance. Several couples occupied cozy tables.

"Did you order?"

Baranovsky nodded, shaking a sweaty hand.

"Only cognac tonight."

Vladik poked his finger in the area of his liver.

"Vodka hasn't been good for me these days."

Vladik ordered an Armenian cognac. Cognac always helped him to relax and refresh his thoughts. Sip by sip, Vladik enjoyed the taste and warmth of the drink, feeling how stress began to leave his body.

"Cognac is a pure product. It won't make you sick."

Baranovsky nodded in agreement with Vladik.

"Any new girls?"

"No worthy ones yet. There were two hookers from Nikolaev, but they say they're busy now. They have a meeting with foreigners at ten o'clock at night."

"That'll be at ten. It's early nine. Call them here."

***

A pretty woman, rustling her slippers on the parquet floor, brought a tray of jasmine tea. There were various kinds of jam in the bowls. Khanya smiled gratefully, sitting on the sofa opposite the gray-haired, military-looking owner of the hut.

"I recommend you try the tea. Our employees brought it from Denmark. Delicious tea!"

Khanya moved closer to the table.

"What about my request? Will you think about it at your leisure?"

"I'll do more than think about it," Khanya took a couple of sips. "I've got some good journalists in mind. Not all of them have indeed had a good life. But they're capable and, most importantly, honest."

"That's right," the host responded vividly. "It is always difficult for an honest person to break through. With us, in the prosecutor's office, this problem is worse than anywhere else. You don't have to tell me, you know, the specifics of the job. Sometimes, it's a shame that a talented person has been shifting papers from folder to folder for years, and some upstart has made it to the top thanks to his acquaintance. The head prosecutor of the republic is one of those. If someone drinks wildly and brings girls to offices, it's normal, but if instead he lectures at the university, they think it's a waste of time. They say: "Disorder! Does he have a lot of free time? Immediately load him with work!" Therefore, we, a group of coworkers, want to prepare keen, timely information for the central press. There's no place in the prosecutor's office for dishonest people with dirty affairs."

"Why are you talking about nothing but work?"

With a smile, a pretty woman addressed the apartment's owner.

"Let the man eat something. How are your parents?"

"Fine, thank you."

"Give our best regards to them from us!"

"I will!"

It's ten o'clock in the evening. Khanya has to go. Should he stay longer? Thanks, but it's late. Besides, he had a lot of work to do, so he was tired. Khanya wanted to sleep. They exchanged the standard, polite parting phrases. A funny poodle brought his sneakers in his teeth. Everyone laughed. Hallway. Front door. Deserted street.

***

By ten o'clock in the evening, Vladik had drunk a bottle and a half of Armenian cognac and, after a hot appetizer, asked for vodka, forgetting about his liver problems. The hookers, smiling stupidly with appetizing lips, began parting.

Vladik did not want to listen to silly female chatter. He said, "Sit!" in a tone that did not tolerate objections and went to look for a waiter. By this time, Baranovsky was already very drunk and obediently nodded his head to the music.

Soon Vladik returned, pushing the waiter with a broken nose and three bottles of vodka. There were no girls at the table.

"Where are the girls?"

Baranovsky reached for the vodka.

"Gone."

"Why did they leave?"

The waiter hid behind the backs of the dancers. Vladik became aggressive after drinking cognac.

"They're meeting the Italians at the hotel entrance at ten."

"Why did you let them go?"

Vladik slapped the boxer's forehead with the palm of his hand. Baranovsky stared at the brown-haired man in fright and surprise.

"They left on their own. I didn't let them go."

"Are we worse than the Italians?"

"No, not worse. We are better than them."

Baranovsky nodded with a heavy chin.

"Don't we have money?"

"We have more money than the Italians."

"So what's the matter? We've been abandoned! I paid for them in the restaurant, and they are seeing the Italians!"

Vladik, staggering, ran downstairs to the restaurant exit.

The girls, flirting with foreigners, got into a brand-new foreign car. While closing the door, the skinny Italian in a white suit smelled a strong odor of alcohol, then a sharp jolt. After that, he fell into a

puddle of unpleasant, sticky water. The drunken brown-haired man methodically pounded his fist into his girlfriend's face.
"Comrade!"
The foreigner began to speak in the language of interethnic communication, but then he fell back into the puddle from which he had just risen after a decisive blow on his chin. Blood rushed to his face.
Turning the brown man around to face him, the skinny man struck his assailant with the back of his fist. Vladik tumbled amusingly, rolling backward to the Press kiosk. A metal object gleamed in his hand. Gunshots. The back window of a foreign car shattered. The Italians jumped into the car. The girls, sobbing fearfully, rushed toward the Republican Stadium. Baranovsky, with trembling hands, put his arms around the brown man's shoulders and dragged him back to the pub. A Browning pistol, a woman's cosmetic bag, and shards of glass were left at the Rus Hotel entrance.
By the time the police patrol arrived (the police were not in a hurry to go where they shoot), passers-by had picked up both the cosmetic bag and the gun. The broken glass was left lying on the road. The police officers drove back to the district office to drink tea and finish their game of cards.

***

An elderly woman with a wand in her right hand slowly entered the restaurant, supported by a girl in a tight-fitting jumpsuit. Seeing Vladik, the girl trembled nervously. Baranovsky rubbed his palms together contentedly:
"Vladik, look, one of the hookers is back."
Vladik swore vigorously, wiping his mouth with the tip of the tablecloth.
"Why did you give her my home phone number?"
Boxer again felt that he had done something wrong.

"Well, they were leaving, and as I don't have a phone, ... I gave them your phone number."

The brown-haired man, swaying, headed towards the elderly woman.

"They were leaving. Now they're back. The only thing missing was my mom."

"Whose mom?"

"Mine. Whose mom? You weren't born a dumb ass for nothing."

From a family and domestic point of view, the elegant brown-haired man could be characterized as a docile, generally obedient son. At the beginning of his life, Vladik was an ideal child. He always helped his mom around the house and dreaded the look of disappointment in her eyes. Vladik's mom was everything to him - a reliable support and the dearest person in the world. But over the years, something changed. He ignored his mom's advice and her demands. And the worst thing was that he started to lie to his mom, covering himself with lies and apologies.

Vladik loved his mom, but he couldn't stand it when his mom started scolding him in front of strangers.

"Sonny, you haven't served all your time in prison for your past crimes. It's a good thing uncle Kostya helped us with the amnesty. So, tell me, what stops you from living like daddy? Why did you shoot at Italians?"

The elderly woman looked reproachfully at her son.

"Mom, do not stop me from resting how I want!" With irritation, replied Vladik.

The elderly woman sat beside her son, taking his hand in her cold palms.

"Dad wouldn't have done that. He would calmly and thoughtfully have sorted everything out. You've been hurt. I can see that. Still, you have to keep your feelings in check."

"Mom, stay out of my soul!"

"Why have you broken that girl's face? Aren't you ashamed? No? Look me in the eye. She has to go to school tomorrow, by the way."
"Don't meddle in my private life!"
"Come on, baby, let's go home. You've had your fun, that's enough. Not every day is a holiday. You've got to be reasonable."
"Mom..."
Baranovsky was left sitting alone. Vladik's mother got hold of her son's arm and took the disorderly "child" home.

***

Khanya heard about what had happened from Rakhit. Vladik and Baranovsky had a very real chance of going to jail. No one knew where the gun, which probably had fingerprints, had gone. Vladik had jeopardized not only himself but the whole gang. Besides, the gun belonged to Oleg. He needed to talk seriously with Vladik about discipline and ethical behavior in public places.
"What time should I schedule a meeting with Vladik?"
Baranovsky mumbled into the phone.
"As soon as I wake up," Khanya answered nervously.
"Can you be more precise?"
"Let's make it noon. Assign him a meeting somewhere in the countryside, away from prying eyes."
"I'll do as you say."
Khanya had always been fascinated by Baran's submissiveness. "He's an interesting man," Khanya thought of the boxer.

***

Vladik was late for the meeting.
"I see you're looking forward to seeing me," he smiled a lusciously kind smile instead of a greeting.
"Look at your watch," Khanya said, stretching his words lazily.

"Fuck you," Vladik said stiffly. "We have no business today. Why did you gather everyone? Do you like to hold party meetings? Your parents aren't communists by any chance, are they?"

Korotyshka blew his nose. He moved to a safe distance just in case. The atmosphere was getting hotter by the minute.

Khanya, without changing his expression, walked right up to the brown-haired man:

"Yes, communists. Just like your parents. Like everyone in this country. Does that give you the right to forget you're just a piece of stuck-up shit? Or is it time to remind you where you belong?"

"Are you going to remind me?"

Vladik laughed in his face.

"You're nothing on your own. When you have as many prison years behind you as I do, then we'll talk. Why? Go on. Take a walk. Okay, I'll let you go."

Vladik barely dodged a sideways right. Ducking under his arm, the brown-haired man drew his knife and stabbed Khanya as hard as possible. The blade slid across his ribs and into his body.

The people around them shrank back like rats before a rush. They waited. That's the way it is in life. Most people take a neutral stance until the winner's name is clear. People are afraid of being cheap. What if they swear allegiance to the wrong person?

Khanya lunged forward piling Vladik on his back, trying to shoulder the knife-wielding arm. Twisting frantically, the brown-haired stabbed Khanya several times from top to bottom. Vladik knew how to handle a knife. It was evident that he had used the knife to argue with his opponent many times before.

While Vladik was faster, Khanya was physically stronger and heavier. He hooked his fingers into the brown-haired man's throat. His pupils dilated with anger when he peered into his opponent's narrowed eyes. Vladik's body went limp. The knife fell from his hands. It was a short, almost lightning-fast fight.

Khanya stood up. Blood was gushing from the wound, but Khanya didn't notice it. Defeating his opponent brought a flood of unparalleled emotion to him. It was a strange feeling with a touch of extreme sexual excitement. Each blow with his fist on his bloody face was like a cock striking inside a woman's body.

If Vadik continued resisting, Khanya would surely keep beating him. Khanya got up and kicked the guy's chest several times with feral ferocity, feeling a sense of pleasure from the accurately delivered blows.

The opponent did not move. With gray foam on his bluish lips, Vladik lay on the asphalt without signs of life. Khanya stopped. He had no purpose to kill. The goal was to break the will, to force obedience. He wanted to punish Vladik, to do it as an example to others. But Vladik stabbed him in front of everyone. He crossed a line that should not be crossed. A bad example for others. Besides, Vladik is vindictive. If he survives, he won't forgive. Vladik will wait for the right moment and stab you in the back, and you can't let that happen.

"Finish him off. Dump his body in the Dnieper, away from the city."

One of the guys approached the brown-haired man cautiously. They kicked him. One. Another. Vladik wheezed. As if awakened from hibernation, the mute witnesses jumped up to him and in a matter of minutes turned his body into bleeding mincemeat mooing unintelligible phrases through tears.

Khanya looked at the crowd silently, disdainfully, and got into the car. Vladik stopped moving and lay without signs of life, but the men kept beating his body.

The ignition switch. The gas pedal. The car with Khanya disappeared round the corner. The beating stopped. There was no one to show loyalty to.

***

Rachit was methodically treating Khanya's wounds.

"Five stab wounds, a lot of cuts. Nothing looks like it's been seriously injured. Is your face okay?"

"Uh, yeah."

Rahit said, jabbing his finger into a rib.

"You'll have to have it stitched. It's a deep gash. You should go to hospital."

"Finished?"

"It's done. That's all I can do. We still have to go to the doctor. The wounds are too deep. We should have shot him right away instead of having a stupid duel. Shall we go to the hospital?"

"Not today."

Khanya shivered and lay down on the bed. - "Bring someone for the good of my soul."

Rakhit wanted to object but changed his mind. He threw his bag over his shoulder and went where he was sent.

Khanya was left alone. The wounds were burning his body from the outside, his thoughts - from the inside. Only now came the proper sense of what had happened. And again, it happened utterly different from what he wanted, with a completely different result. This was not what he had wished to, not this! How could he have gotten this far? And most importantly - everything that happened was senseless. Khanya was getting angrier and angrier at himself. The doorbell rang. From afar came voices of girls and Rakhit. Khanya thought of disgusted people, not wanting to see Rakhit or those he had brought. An old street joke came to mind:

"Tell me, are there any women not for sale?"

"Of course there are, but they are costly."

"Everything sells for money. Everything is inferior to power," Khanya thought as he looked at the cracks in the ceiling. "Greed is the true engine of human history."

Smiling smugly, Khanya felt like Napoleon.

Pain, ordinary human pain, tart and burning, brought his thoughts back to earth and made him remember who he was and who he really is. The guests stood for a while on the staircase and left. Like clouds driven by the wind, Khanya's thoughts were bustling by an effort of will, floating somewhere far away, dissolving behind the room's walls. How pleasant it is to lie in a warm bed. How nice to be silent. How nice not to think.

CHAPTER III

A young woman hurried out of the supermarket, laden with bags of groceries. There are many women like her on the streets of cities. Always in a hurry, tired of everyday routine and hard work. Such women are genuinely happy about little things. The most interesting thing is that in some ways they are much happier than we are.
Khanya bumped into a woman in the doorway of a supermarket, almost knocking a milk carton out of her hands. Habitually he threw, "Excuse me," and ducked into the back of the store.
"Oleg," her voice called, filled with tenderness and warmth.
Khanya flinched in surprise. What a familiar voice! He looked back. Perhaps the girl was confused?
"Oleg," repeated the lips.
A smile. Fluffy blond hair. The eyes inexorably calling to the past.
"I'm sorry. I didn't recognize you."
Lena placed the bag on top of the grocery bag. The woman standing in front of him looked completely different from the one who had come out of the underpass to meet him long ago, on the eighth of March. The girl he had first given flowers to. She was the girl he first kissed. Everything was for the first time with her.
"I've changed a lot, haven't I?"

Khanya looked sadly at the tattered shopping bags. He wanted to lie, but he couldn't.

"It's really true. Let me help you."

Together they went outside. There was a ring glittering on Lena's hand.

"How long have you been married?"

"About two years. Exactly as long as I had been awaiting you from the army, despite your insistent requests to forget. Those were your requests."

"You remember even that."

"It took me too long to get over the idea that you weren't going to come back, even though I realized it was foolish to await you." Lena stopped.

"I have to take the streetcar." After a minute, she said: "Come to visit me. I live nearby, on Komarov Avenue."

"With your husband?"

"With my husband and my daughter."

"You have a daughter? Congratulations."

"Thank you. You really should come over. I'm home all day." - And timidly asked: "Will you write down my phone number?"

On a piece of paper, a few numbers. Like before. As if it were yesterday.

***

Taking out his apartment keys, Khanya didn't immediately notice that a man in a roughly knitted sweater was waiting for him outside his apartment.

"Where have you been all morning?"

Khanya looked up questioningly at Gosha's disheveled head.

"You look like something's happened."

"Did you know it would turn out this way? No, just give me the answer - did you know?"

"Knew what? What are you asking me? Calm down!"

Khanya stepped aside and leaned towards Rakhit, who was standing nearby.

"What's wrong with Gosha? Why is he so nervous today?"

Rakhit shrugged nervously.

"Lord has returned from the Crimea. He's come back alone."

***

A man with a soft and tired voice was having lunch at the apartment of a girl he knew. A sixteen-year-old girl in long shorts stood between him and the gas stove. When Oleg entered the kitchen, Lord, having snatched a hefty piece of chicken leg with his teeth, greeted him with a glance.

"You should lock the front door," Khanya said, sitting at the table.

"Why? Whoever needs it will find a way to get in," - Blond took his eyes off the chicken. – "By the way, how's the brown-haired man's health? I haven't seen him lately."

There was a strange note in Lord's voice. Khanya looked around warily.

"Not bad. Why?"

"Nothing. You did the right thing. I would have washed Vladik's slobbering face in the toilet long ago." Sigh: "You beat me to it. I approve."

"You don't seem very cheerful."

"Why not? The sea air has done me good. Want some tea?"

"Uh, no."

"Coffee, then?

"I heard you came alone."

Blond leaned back in the kitchen chair.

"You heard right."

"Where's Slon?"

"Swimming in the sea. He liked swimming in Yalta."

"What's that supposed to mean?"

Lord finished his tea. Put his feet in his sneakers.

"I'm responsible for the people I brought into business. He came with me, and he left with me," Blond stood up. "Are you leaving or staying?" Pointing at the girl's thighs with his eyes. "I recommend getting to know her better."

The fellows went outside. Blond headed towards the intersection. "By the way," shoving his hands into the spacious pockets of his jeans, he carelessly said to Oleg, "Slon's nervous system turned out to be entirely unsuitable for really serious business. You, like me, don't need extra headache, do you?"

Khanya nodded his head faintly in agreement. Getting into the car, he said to Rakhit:

"Drive first to Stalinka and from there to the center."

Tears were silently streaming down Rakhit's face. Khanya was confused by the surprise. Instinctively, he put his hand on the driver's shoulder.

"Yura, what's wrong with you?"

"Slon was my friend."

The car started to move.

That same evening, without saying a word to anyone, the man with the soft and tired voice left Kiev.

***

A heavy, pressurized feeling restrained the movements of his arms and legs and bound his thoughts. Khanya could not relax despite all his efforts. He sat in the darkened room, trying to release himself from the heaviness in his soul. His strong arms were trembling now as if he were but a puppet in the hands of fate. Only faint streaks of light penetrated the room through the thick curtains, creating a feeling of emptiness and loneliness.

Khanya raised the glass of whiskey to his lips and took a sip, but even the sharp taste of alcohol couldn't ease his tension. He was having more and more nightmares at night, and he couldn't wish anything away.

Khanya stood up and began pacing around the room, trying to dispel the darkness within him. His fists clenched and unclenched as if he was fighting an invisible enemy. It seemed to him that every step and movement was meant to help him free himself from this oppressive atmosphere, but nothing comforted him.

What was the taste of safety and peace? He could not remember. It had been too long since he experienced those feelings while balancing the precipice. To fully rest and recover, Oleg needed to forget about the danger. He couldn't relax with alcohol, it was too primitive.

His gaze fell on a crumpled piece of paper. An open window. The purple glow of the street lamps on the walls of the houses. The telephone. Long beeps. Short phrases. Scraps of crumpled thoughts.

"Come over. I'm waiting for you," at the other end of the phone call.

***

Khanya found the apartment rather quickly. The door was not opened for a long time. After hesitating, Khanya rang the doorbell again. Again, no one opened the door. Khanya turned around to leave, and at that moment the door opened.

"I thought you weren't home."

Instead of greeting, Lena smiled affectionately:

"I was on the balcony. I didn't hear you call right away," she closed the front door and entered the room.

"I can't believe you remembered me after all. You came..."

Khanya's gaze slid around the apartment. A narrow room, a kitchen that was cramped even for him alone. The only joy was the telephone and the balcony. But what's the point? In a cage like this.

"You don't even have a TV."

Lena shrugged guiltily.

"Not yet. I'm fine without a TV."
"I should get you one."
She laughed:
"Where am I going to put it?" She sat down on the sofa. "Better tell me how you live."
On the balcony - a stroller, children's things on the rope. Oleg sank down next to Lena. Inhaling the smell of hair, he remembered the girl with blond hair from the years gone by, remembered her groaning "Why?" when she was lying on the bed, and he first entered her. It had been a first for both him and her then.
Lena ran her hand gently over the back of his head:
"How wonderful it is to feel as if you're seventeen again."
Oleg put his head in her lap.
"I am experiencing a feeling of guilt. I treated you unfairly and cruelly."
"That's in the past. Did you find the girl you were looking for?"
Oleg remembered how Lena cried when she found out that he was simultaneously dating her and other girls. There was not a word of reproach from her. Only silent tears.
"With you, I felt much freer than when I was alone. That's true."
A sad, muffled sigh in response. Lena got up to see if the baby was asleep.
"Lena, how do you feel about your husband?"
"I love him," she answered in an even, impassive voice. "He's a very good man. I would never hurt him."
"May I have a look?"
"Sure."
Oleg opened the family album. Weekdays. A wedding. A housewarming. A crowd of relatives. Gala dinner. Weekdays. In the pictures, everybody smiles, all are happy. But in real life...
"What's happening to us all?" - Khanya mentally asked himself. He didn't realize whether he was glad or not that he had come to Lena, that he had met his first love again. It was an unconscious

attempt to return to the past, to return to the place to which there was no turning back.

Lena's husband made no impression on Khanya. Just an ordinary country boy. He wanted to ask: "Couldn't you find anyone better?"

"He loves me and is a wonderful dad."

Lena had an amazing quality. She could hear him without words.

"That's the main thing," Khanya closed the album. "Are you happy?"

"I have everything I dreamed of. Happiness is to have a home of your own, a family that loves you and waits for you when you come home after work."

"Huh?...? That's not enough."

"Maybe. Not enough for you, more than enough for me."

Lena put a strong-brewed coffee on the coffee table.

"You've changed, Oleg."

"Is it noticeable?"

"Very. Not so much outwardly but inside. You've become more withdrawn; you've become more rigid. You weren't like this before."

Lena touched his cheek with her palm. She laughed:

"Like a hedgehog, prickly."

Oleg slowly kissed her fingertips.

"What was I for you?"

The girl wondered:

"Why was? You're a part of my life. You know, after you left me, I could not come to my senses for a long time. Tried to forget, wanted to erase from my memory everything that was connected with you. Then I realized it was stupid. You can't change the past. But I'm grateful that you were in it."

"The past can come back."

He drew her to him, sliding his hands down her thighs. Lena gently pulled away from him.

"The past doesn't come back. Sometimes, the future is like the past days, but I don't want that anymore. Too much has changed since then. What can you offer me? To be a wife? I wouldn't let my daughter be without a father. To be a mistress? Occasionally seeing you in secret? Such a position is humiliating to me."

"The evident conclusion: I mean nothing to you," Oleg said with irritation. "Like a nonentity."

Oleg could not stand it when women denied him affection.

Lena sank to the floor at Oleg's feet.

"Why are you talking so? You know how good I feel with you. I wish... I'd really like us to remain friends and you to come to us sometimes, just like that."

A quiet, barely audible baby sob came from behind the balcony door. Lena nimbly jumped up and ran to the baby's stroller. Oleg clearly realized that he did not belong there. Before Khanya stood a complete stranger, a stranger woman with a half-asleep, cute, and yet alien to him child. Only her eyes, tired and languid, reminded him of the girl he had once loved.

Khanya took a funny plush piggy toy from a plastic bag and put it on the coffee table next to the empty cups. He got up.

"Leaving?"

Their eyes met.

"I gotta go."

"Will you come again to see me?"

Hope in the question, mute words: "Don't go. Please. Not now."

"I'll give you a call."

He knew he would never call again.

In the doorway:

"Oleg!"

Khanya turned around. The chubby baby's mouth was smiling serenely, looking at the unfamiliar man.

"This child could have been yours."

***

Oleg absent-mindedly looked at the passing cars and thought about how and why beautiful, slender girls literally in a few short years turn into shapeless pieces of meat? Whence and why instead of the smell of spring flowers after the morning rain there are smells of rot, rotten fish and decay? Why does Time so ruthlessly quickly change the female body and as if in mockery of a woman leaves her soul unchanged?

Oleg went through the memory of images, shades of feelings, departed dreams. What is love? Sacrament given by God? Animal instinct, sweet pain tearing the thickness of time that separates modern civilization from the primordial cry? Remember them all - the women whose warmth warmed you, at whose knees you bowed as if before an altar! What did you realize when you kissed their hot lips?

Faces, hands, bodies flashed in your subconsciousness with the bright glare of scattered photographs.... Voices, barely perceptible. Distinct. Different voices, like the glow of dew on coastal rocks.

"Love is a constant search for a partner, a search for a stream of hitherto unexperienced feelings that lift us to Heaven..."

"...it's just a job that you want to finish quickly, take the money and leave..."

"...colored by third-rate lyrics to satisfy the physiological needs of the body..."

"The ultimate goal of sexual intercourse is not marriage, not procreation, but aspiration to grasp the wisdom of the Creator through what we call love. A fusion, a plunge into infinity where there is neither death nor life. Wet happy eyes. The mutual attraction of bodies."

Voices decreasing and then increasing, faded out, drowning in a single stream, reminiscent of the murmur of the surf beyond the horizon line. If you close your eyes and put your hands over your ears, you will hear this noise inside you, in the labyrinth where thoughts hide.

***

Korotyshka threw his pocket mirror at the doorjamb with fury. "You think you can break anyone? You're trying for nothing, bitch. You won't succeed." The shards rolled under the couch with a tinkling sound. The cold air rushed through his swollen gums with a tart pain-coolness, wheezing out.

Rather than physical pain, it was the resentment that choked his chest and made Korotyshka suffer. He couldn't forgive Khanya for knocking his teeth out in front of everyone. Outwardly it looked as if Korotyshka had accepted it, but in his heart, he held a grudge. He couldn't, shouldn't have been treated that way. That's what Korotyshka thought, and in his own way, he was right. Especially now, after what had happened to Vladik, who was considered Khanya's right-hand man.

The Brown-haired wasn't just an ordinary errand boy. He belonged to an influential Kiev group that was once part of Khanya's structure. Who was Khanya anyway? Nobody knew about him when Vladik first went to prison and gained respect among the prisoners. How come Vladik's men rushed to kill him at Khanya's first command? Gosha's men were understandable, but Baranovsky.... Korotyshka didn't understand how Khanya could dare to make a show trial. Well, Vladik was wrong about something - so they could talk and have a drink or two.... But to kill in front of everyone!

Vladik had known Khanya for over three years. A broad-shouldered brunet with a good-natured smile and a rather tough character made a favorable impression at the moment of acquaintance. They were united by their dislike for Ahmed according to the principle: "Enemies of my enemies are my friends", and then by common affairs. At first, Khanya acted through Vladik, giving his boys work. Vladik distributed the profits among his boys himself. After a while, it became clear to everyone that it was much more profitable to work directly with Khanya than through the Brown-haired. Vladik had neither fresh ideas nor ability to analyze the situation analytically. Moreover, he never fully understood how it had happened that Khanya had taken over the power in his gang.

***

The Pleshyvyi was strolling with Baranovsky in front of the entrance to the Rus Hotel.
"Personally, I feel sorry for Vladik," the boxer cautiously probed his companion with sly eyes from under his eyebrows.
The companion waved his hand indifferently:
"Regret it not, but Vladik couldn't get anything else. Khanya needed silent performers, not potential competitors. All he needed was an excuse. Any excuse. Khanya got it and used it. True, not in the best way, but he got what he wanted. No more Vladik getting in the way. You, by the way, were always the closest to Vladik."
Baranovsky shrugged warily:
"Me? What's that got to do with me? He and I were never close friends." - He hesitated: "I just don't understand why Khanya didn't do it sooner."
"What's so incomprehensible? Someone had to fight Ahmed. Besides, even with repeat offenders in Khanya's entourage, the Caucasian had Khanya cornered. That's all changed now. Ahmed is out of the way. Apparently, Khanya decided it was time to make a purge among his own people. Let others be afraid."
Baranovsky nodded his head in agreement and thought to himself: "Today it's Vladik and who will be tomorrow? Khanya is becoming more and more paranoid, seeing everyone as an enemy. He's becoming unpredictable and dangerous to everyone."

CHAPTER IV

In late August 1990, a wave of apartment burglaries swept through the new districts of Kiev, such as Troyeshchina, Obolon, and partially through Kharkivsky district. The ensuing lull, which coincided with the beginning of active police searches, spoke either of the thieves' good knowledge or of the gang leader's extraordinary intuition.

While the investigators were wondering who it could be, Khanya, analyzing the nature of the thefts, realized that the rumors about Nurik's release from prison were true.

Nurik (in the world Stanislav Nurmagomedov) had served time in prison for two convictions at once - for burglary and petty hooliganism. He was released on the twentieth day of June. For a month or so, Nurik vacationed at the seaside, then he returned to Kyiv. Nurik's return to Kyiv after his release from prison was felt by the locals.

Unremarkable, below average height, with a pimply, perpetually swollen face, as if from overdrinking or chronic sleep deprivation, Nurik resembled something like a lowered, drunken engineer (by his grip and perpetually disgruntled expression) or a relative of the head of a commodity warehouse. Nurik dressed tastelessly but in everything new - imported and expensive.

- Don't look that I'm small - I'm all in my penis, - Nurik bragged to a stupid hooker, a finalist of the beauty contest "Miss Kiev."

To this statement, his buddy remarked half-voiced:

- Because of drugs, your dick had already forgotten when it went up on women, except for dangling from the draught in the restroom.

Nurik took the friendly remark as an expression denigrating his good name. Without a second thought, he plunged a knife into his buddy. After that, he apologized for a long time, explaining that there had been a ridiculous misunderstanding and that he had misunderstood who and what he had said between the second bottle of vodka and the decanter of Armenian brandy. The knife was removed. The buddy was taken to hospital, and his life was saved. The hooker was fucked. Everyone had a pleasant and fun time.

***

Marina leaned over the crib, her heart beating so loudly that it seemed it might burst out of her chest. The little boy was lying in a fever; his face was covered with sweat, and he blinked restlessly in his sleep. In his half-sleeping delirium, he threw his arms about, whispered inarticulate words, and often shrieked through nervous sobs. Marina felt her own hands trembling as she tried to lay her son on his back to ease his breathing.

At the slightest rustle in the stairwell, Marina rose on tiptoe and rushed to the front door. Her heart pounded frantically in her chest as she hoped to hear the sound of an ambulance creaking, but the silence only grew, and that tormented her the most. "Why is the 'ambulance' taking so long?" - The blood pulsed in her temples, and Marina began chewing her nails in anticipation.

"Mom... ma..." - whispered a weak voice from the crib.

The baby's fingers wrapped around Marina's neck, and she pressed her son against her as if that could provide him with some relief.

"It hurts, Mommy," the little voice whispered again.

"Be patient, my good man," Marina pressed him even tighter. – "You are patient, aren't you? Soon, a doctor will come and give you a pill, and you will be fine."

Marina stroked the small palm of her son and tried to smile, although the glint in her eyes was tears.

"Bitter?" Asked the child with heavy eyelids that fought sleep and sickness.

"No, the most delicious one!" Marina tried to make her voice soft and comforting. "And when you recover, we'll go to the toy store, and I'll give you the world's best steam train. Deal?"

The boy smiled weakly, and Marina realized that even in his condition, he understood her words. Her heart squeezed with pain and helplessness, but she had to stay strong for her son.

She bit her lip to keep from crying in front of him. The ambulance was due any minute, and she hoped the doctor would bring relief to her child. At this moment, she was willing to do anything to make her son feel better.

The child clung even more tightly to his mother. Tears, hot tears of silent crying flowed down his cheeks. The doorbell rang.

***

Oksana had been working as a part-time ambulance paramedic for a number of years. At first, it was very hard. In addition, she had to balance her work and her studies at medical school. But over time, Oksana got used to this rhythm, realizing that the noble profession of a doctor requires she have not only knowledge but also an endless willingness to help others.

Usually, there were three of them - she, a young guy after college and a serious lady of forty years old who liked to ask pedantically about the patient's health before prescribing treatment. Being a high-class specialist, this woman was a kind of supervisor for Oksana, always vigilant about the quality of medical care.

The supervisor trusted Oksana, which was a great honor for her. That's why when the supervisor called Oksana one day before her shift, she was not surprised.

"Oksana," she asked. "Can you manage without me today? For family reasons, I have to take the day off."

"Everything will be fine. Don't worry," Oksana answered, trying to calm down the supervisor.

"Oksana, you know I always worry. Human lives depend on our work. If there is a severe case, come and pick me up. In the morning, don't forget to tell me how the night shift went."

"Yes, yes, of course," - Oksana exhaled, putting down the receiver. Her heart squeezed with the responsibility she felt for each patient.

Her partner, absent-mindedly leafing through a collection of detective stories, took his eyes off the book:

"She's dumping all the work on us today?"

Her son came on leave from the army. He's been in the army for a year.

"Ah..."

"What do you mean, "ah..."? You have yet to serve in the army."

Her colleague sniffed his nose indifferently.

"We'll see. Maybe I'll go to the institute, and won't have to serve in the army."

There were only two calls before midnight, and both of them were successfully handled. At about one o'clock in the morning, when the whole city was asleep, and only the sounds of night silence broke the monotonous muttering of telephone lines, they went to Nivki. They found the house and the right entrance quickly. The door was opened by a young woman with tearful eyes. There was a baby lying in the crib, and Oksana realized that it was an emergency.

At first glance, Oksana determined that the condition of the little patient was very serious and required urgent hospitalization. She quickly asked:

"What are you complaining about?"

"Temperature 38.2, severe pain in the navel area - answered the child's mother. - Nausea, there was vomiting."

"It's a familiar voice. Where could I have heard it before?" - Oksana carefully looked at the child's mother. Maybe... No... Exactly. Her!

Oksana clearly remembered a bright, spectacularly dressed girl with luxurious hair who approached her at the metro station "Khreschatyk." She believed the stranger and received a spray of gas in the face from an unshaven man. Oksana remembered how her husband and mother yelled at her instead of sympathy, how the policeman listened to her indifferently, with a smirk, and how the man with the reek of alcohol gasped in her ear: "If you scream, I'll kill you!" She remembered her fingers hurting so long after the mugger had torn off her rings in a hurry.

Biting her lips, Oksana was no longer thinking about the baby. A hot wave of hatred mixed with animal fear spilled over her body. The child's sobbing, Marina's tears, and the miserably furnished room gave rise to a strange feeling of irritation and gloating delight.

"The usual poisoning. Children often have it," Oksana said in a cold, alien voice. Just as nonchalantly, she gave the child's mother painkillers.

"If the stomach hurts a lot, put a heating pad on it."

"Thank you, doctor... Thank you very much," Marina whispered quietly to people in white coats. In the hallway, she discreetly put some crumpled bills into the paramedic's pocket as a token of gratitude. Oksana did not say anything but coldly nodded her head in farewell.

On the way back, Oksana did not utter a word. A strange, wandering smile slipped an invisible shadow, hiding in her eyes. She thought to herself: "You will be punished by your own child." She remembered the child. So what? There's nothing strange in the fact that the ambulance on duty made a wrong diagnosis. It happens a lot in medical practice.

***

Marina was rushing around the apartment. The child was getting worse and worse. In the morning, a sharp exacerbation occurred.

Another ambulance team which arrived in the morning unmistakably diagnosed acute appendicitis. When the crying mother with the boy in her arms was taken to the hospital, it became clear that urgent surgery was no longer necessary.

"If you had come at least a few hours earlier," was all the doctor on duty could say, nervously wiping his thick, clumsy-rimmed glasses.

***

Nurik liked to eat delicious food. While eating, various thoughts came to mind, interesting, fresh ideas, and it was possible to draw interesting conclusions. Nurik was amused by the drops of sweat on Semyon Davydovich's forehead. The owner of the cafe clearly did not want to part with his money.

"What does this have to do with me? Guys, you'll work something out among yourselves. I can't pay everyone."

"You don't have to pay everybody. You'll pay only us," - Nurik said judiciously chewing a Kiev-style cutlet.

"Didn't you understand it well?"

The heavy hand of Nurik's friend lay on the restaurant owner's shoulder. Semyon Davydovich flinched. Manyunya's colorless eyes looked through his interlocutor with a blank, emotionless stare.

"Maybe you're not glad we're back?"

"There was nothing I could do. Who am I? A little man. You disappeared. Khanya came and started demanding money."

"Nobody cares about that," Hasan joined the conversation.

"Whether Ahmed is there or not is a third question. Did you pay?" Hasan smiled.

"Good. You can keep paying, only with your own money. It shouldn't affect our money. We didn't break the contract with you. Or did you break it without us?"

"No. No way," whispered Semyon Davydovich fearfully.

"Then pay up."

"And Khanya?"

"They'll deal with him without your participation."

The restaurant's guards were selected directly by Gosha. The guy standing at the door sensed that something was wrong when a group of tightly bunched visitors of athletic type went to Semyon Davydovich's locker room.

"Do you need help?" He took a moment to ask Semyon Davydovich.

"It's all right," the cafe owner waved his hand fidgetily. "I'll call you if I need you."

Soon, the phone rang in Gosha's apartment. Gosha reluctantly turned down the sound of the television. He picked up the phone and listened lazily.

"Okay, don't panic. I'll send Korotyshka over. He will quickly find out what's going on there."

Without much desire, more out of habit, he dialed a familiar number. He talked to Korotyshka and immediately forgot about everything, staring at the blue screen. There was an interesting movie on TV.

Korotyshka arrived at the moment when the uninvited guests were leaving the cafe. He had never met Nurik before, but he recognized Manyunya and Hasan at once. Chillingly, he watched the guests leisurely getting into their cars, having finished their cigarettes. It was as if neither Ahmed's disappearance nor the forced expulsion of his supporters had happened. What is the reason for such an unexpected return? Do they not realize the danger? Is it elementary carelessness or something else? Korotyshka sensed that something had changed, and it was not for his better, but what exactly had happened, he could not understand at that moment. Fear, penetrating deep into his body through his fingertips, enveloped his heart in a fog.

Nurik and Ahmed's former associates were long gone. Now nothing threatened Korotyshka's safety, but he did not dare to get out of the car.

***

Dozens of phone calls pierced Khanya's eardrums with sharp wedges. Guys in leather jackets crowded into the kitchen, Gosha smoked cigarette after cigarette by the window, and the telephone brought more and more news.
Ahmed's associates had rallied around Nurik. Having waited for the right moment, they reminded about themselves in all the key points that had previously belonged to Ahmed and brought the most significant part of the profits. Four of Khanya's boys were brutally beaten. A broker who worked for Khanya was picked up with a stab wound near Republic Stadium. The windows in Kudryavy's central video salon were blown down by machine gun fire.

***

Khanya listened calmly to the reports, making notes in his notebook.
"Gosha, did you know Nurik well?"
"What do you mean, well?" He glittered his eyes from under his wheat eyebrows. "Well, we bumped into each other on small things. I thought Nurik would stay out of Kiev with Ahmed's guys. I wonder where he found Manyunya."
"Nurik grew up with Hasan," came a voice from the kitchen.
Khanya got up.
"We should have killed them then," Gosha grinned gloatingly.
The phone rang again.
"Khanya, Nurik is looking for you."
Oleg looked back at the door. Threw his jacket on his shoulders.
"All the better."

***

Nurik counted the money, rolling a smoking cigarette from one corner of his mouth to the other.

"I've been meaning to ask you for a long time, Hasan, who is Khanya? What are they all so afraid of? I don't remember him."

"He's too young for you to remember him," - the Caucasian spat through his teeth.

"Serious people came to Kiev, hiding from the police. They made him strong. Khanya was something like a screen behind which they hid their real names. These people did all the work; the locals thought it was Khanya. Then, somehow, he fooled his bosses and became the boss himself. He was smart enough to do it. Khanya's business profits were very good."

"There is something I don't understand, Hasan," Nurik interrupted him. "Was he in jail or not?"

"No."

"Then what are we talking about? He's a nobody! They'd break him in prison in no time. I can't imagine how you could let a sucker with his gang of sportsmen and teenagers tax half of Kiev and become so brazen as to start telling criminals what they should or shouldn't do."

"Ahmed could not understand it either."

"Ahmed is a separate case. He got greedy and got his hands full. He imagined himself as some unattainable peak of the Caucasus. In his youth, Ahmed would not have made such a mistake. By the way, someone among his people must have betrayed Ahmed. He was taken out too cleanly. People don't usually just disappear like that."

Hiding the money in a filthy plastic pouch, Nurik stuffed it behind the empty bottles in the sideboard.

"Did the guys find out where Khanya is hiding?"

"They're looking."

"Hurry them up. The longer the case drags on, the more unprofitable it becomes."
"It won't. We'll find out everything for money."
Hasan didn't doubt it.

***

Just think how interesting human life is! People are ready to do anything for money, and nothing human is alien to them. It seems that's what Karl Marx, the apologist of communism, wrote. And this applies to absolutely all aspects of social life. Including church life.

On a sweltering September day in 1990, in Moscow region, when the nature seemed calm and unapproachable, a murder occurred that horrified the local population and left many questions unanswered. Archpriest Alexander Men, a man who had devoted his life to faith and spiritual search, became the victim of a heinous crime. The killer, as it was later found out, chose an axe as the murder weapon, and this decision opened the door to a world of monstrous secrets and dark mysteries.

The forest path leading to the Semkhoz platform in Zagorsky district of Moscow region remained little explored, and a sudden blow of the axe to the back of the archpriest's head was a verdict. His last prayers went unheard, and the world lost a man who was honored and respected not only in church circles.

The investigation was going on continuously, and the police were working out one version after another. The possibility of a religious motive was one of the main versions, but it soon faded into the background. The people surrounding the priest only confirmed his kindness and lack of enemies, which greatly complicated the search for the criminal.

Local residents, whose fate was intertwined with the life of the archpriest, worried every day that the murderer remained undiscovered. The village began to miss his wise words and blessings. The bereavement overwhelmed everyone.

Investigators and detectives worked countless hours on the case, but the answers were elusive, like the haze over the thick trees of the forest. With each passing day, the case of the opposition between the unseen killer and the persistent laws became more and more mysterious.

The story of Archpriest Alexander Men became a mystery that remained unsolved. The judicial authorities accumulated a lot of materials, but they could not solve the mystery. The murder of Alexander Men remained a black page in the history of this quiet corner of Moscow region.

Meanwhile, the man who had raised his hand against the priest was not in hiding. Whether or not did the investigators know, but a week after the murder, Kalina knew the name of the perpetrator and his exact location. The murderer did not expect the death of the theologian-writer to cause such a resonance around the world. He trembled with fear, not realizing exactly how it would end.

In his time, Lord had often heard about Alexander Men from Khanya. Khanya had admired the priest, often rereading his six-volume study of the nature and essence of faith, published at various times in Brussels.

Unlike Khanya, the man with the soft and tired voice had no idea how he could have the patience to read six volumes, let alone write a single book. As a matter of fact, he personally didn't give a damn about who wrote what. Nevertheless, sitting in the Three Legs café and recalling how Khanya had characterized Alexander Men, Lord asked Kalina about the murder. The latter smiled condescendingly:

"Why do you need to know something that doesn't concern your affairs?"

"Vitya, I don't care who did it, but I want to believe that such people should not have enemies."

"Everybody has enemies. It's a question of degree. We live in the world that is inherently hostile to us. I believe that the man who killed Alexander Men repents for what he had done. But that doesn't matter. He is doomed if his bosses are those who I think of. They favor his death."

"Are there such people?"

"Don't you know it? Do you think there's peace and quiet within the church walls? Do you believe that the only thing that people there do is pray to God? You'll see, there will be others after this death. Some deaths we will know about, others will not be written about in the newspapers or told on TV. In fact, we all have one road to nether world. Let's have a drink."

They sat at the dinner table. An obliging waitress brought them hot dishes. People are always people and nothing human is alien to them.

***

The December evening on the banks of the Moskva River was imbued with somber atmosphere. Father Lazar, a member of the commission investigating the murder of Archpriest Alexander Men, had become nervous in the past few days and often said that he had missed something. He felt that there were more details to be uncovered in the case of the priest's death.

A week after the last meeting of the commission on December 26, 1990, when everyone thought that the case had slowly but surely come to a solution, one of the neighbors of the priest called the police in the evening. According the police officer who took the call, the voice sounded tense:

"Something is wrong in Priest Lazar's apartment. The door won't close, and the window is dark."

Under the canopy of night, the police officers and investigators arrived at Father Lazar's apartment. The door was ajar, and the night inside was pitch black. The official version - murder for the purpose of robbery - was on the surface, and it was this first impression that served as justification for sorting out the events in the apartment.

However, the deeper the investigators penetrated into the apartment, the more incomprehensible and strange the circumstances became. All valuables that could have attracted a burglar remained in place. In the room where they found the body of Father Lazar, there was ominous silence.

Lazar, 44 years old, was murdered in his bachelor apartment. Dozens of knife cuts, ligature marks, and bruises were found on his body. They found unfinished bottles of alcohol in the kitchen.

All efforts of the investigators were focused on this case as a usual robbery, although their gut feeling suggested that it was not so simple. Other versions that could explain what had happened in Father Lazar's house were not worked out.

Two months later, on February 2, 1990, priest Sergei Shlykov, 33, also known as Hegumen Seraphim, was murdered in his bachelor apartment in Moscow. Shlykov worked in the Department of External Church Relations, served in Israel, first in Jaffa, then in Jerusalem, and in Moscow, and was appointed rector of the Church of Nativity of the Blessed Virgin in Putinki. There were numerous bruises on his body. He died from several blunt blows to the head. An open bottle of champagne was found next to the bed.

In both cases, it was unclear how the killers got into the apartment. According to everyone who knew them, the deceased were very cautious people.

The killers were never found, of course.

CHAPTER V

Rakhit went down into the semi-basement. The light bulb above the stairs shone so dimly that he had to search for the right apartment by feel.
Behind the massive oak doors with pre-revolutionary deadbolts, half a dozen men from Khanya's gang were hanging around in a thick cloud of tobacco smoke. Empty vodka and beer bottles and crumbs of bread were lying underfoot. The pungent odor of cheap women's perfume and sweaty clothes hit Rakhit in the face.
Rakhit walked deep into the apartment, into a small room with a single window overlooking the courtyard.
"Oleg."
Khanya listened tensely to the gray-haired man talking expressively to someone on the phone. Judging from the scraps of phrases coming to Rakhit, the gray-haired man had recently been released from prison.
"Oleg."
Khanya raised his head tiredly.
"I have unpleasant news." After a pause. "Baranovsky and his athletes went over to Nurik's side. He betrayed you and gave them the address of your apartment."
"What now?"
"They didn't find you, and out of impotent rage, they started a fire. You no longer have a place to live except for the charred walls."
"Books?"
That is a naive question. Paper burns fastest.
"There's nothing left in there."
Khanya stood up. He said nonchalantly:
"Let's go."

***

The water pressure slowly extinguished the flames that had erupted in the apartment of the silent brown-haired man. The neighbors watched sympathetically as the firemen carefully inspected the room. The air in the apartment was filled with the smell of burning and gray smoke curls bursting out the windows as if telling about the terrible tragedy that had occurred here.

Soon, accompanied by his friend, the fellow who owned the ruined apartment stepped into the entryway. His look was tired and sad as if he had lost his home and a part of his soul. The neighbors took heart in his grief, and their eyes reflected sincere sympathy.

One of the neighbors, an old man leaning on his cane, said

"We heard about what happened," he said in a low voice. – "It's a pity it happened. How are you feeling?"

"Thank you for asking. It's good that no one was hurt, but ... All my stuff, including my favorite books, burned."

The guy's friend nodded as if confirming his words. The neighbors, listening to their conversation, felt the moment's gravity. They said that the apartment had been robbed, and then, covering their tracks, the robbers poured fuel on the walls and set it on fire. Nothing in the apartment survived.

"We're here to help," said the woman with the blooming geraniums on the windowsill. – "Whatever you need, don't hesitate to ask."

Khanya nodded silently in gratitude and entered the apartment. What could a neighbor in cheap old slippers do for him? Besides books, a large amount of money in cash was hidden in the bookcases. There was so much money that it no longer fit in the bookcases and the hiding place under the sofa.

***

The things that surround us really become part of our world. They take on significance and become an integral part of our daily lives as if giving us a sense of comfort and coziness. Khanya had always known that things were important, but he hadn't realized how much they had deepened in his mind until he saw the destroyed apartment.

The fire had left behind a trail of destruction and disappointment. The flames had devoured not only material possessions but also a part of his inner world. He stood in the middle of this desolate room, where coziness and comfort used to reign, and felt lost.

The walls he knew by heart had become alien and lifeless. The ceiling that used to hide secrets and dreams above him now seemed like blackened evidence of a terrible event. The dirt and ruins left behind by the fire seemed insurmountable obstacles to recovery.

Rakhit, realizing that words could not comfort his friend, gently tried to support him. He knew that nothing would replace the things he had lost, but he was there to support his friend in this difficult moment. So, leaving Khanya in the ruined apartment, he stealthily walked outside.

"I'd better wait for him in the car," the driver thought and breathed a sigh of relief as he stepped out into the yard.

***

Khanya shuddered in surprise at the unnatural sound of the phone ringing in the midst of the ruins. Had he imagined it? No. The phone was actually working. The shattered phone case was covered in black cinder and dirt.

"Hello..."

Silence. Through the creaking wires came a muffled voice: "Oleg..." Khanya squatted down with disgust at what had once been called parquet but was now soiled with the footprints of dozens of shoes. Why did he hear that voice at this very moment, not earlier?

The uninvited guests had found neither the records with the financial calculations nor the money itself. But the fire did. Khanya hid notebooks with notes and money converted into American dollars in the apartment. Yesterday a millionaire, today a beggar. Khanya smiled crookedly to himself.
He put the telephone receiver to his lips.
"I'm listening. Go ahead."
"Did you recognize me?"
"Yes, Letta."
Pause. Then:
"Aren't you glad?"
"Glad."
"I got married."
"Congratulations. How long ago?"
"About 40 minutes. The wedding's tonight."
After a moment's hesitation, she asked again:
"Aren't you glad I called?"
"Why not? It's nice that you remember me. Even if it's after the ceremony at City Hall."
"I want to see you."
"Are you inviting me to the wedding?"
"No. Pick me up after the wedding."
"You want me to steal you?"
"Why steal? I'll go out on my own. If you come, of course."
Khanya thought for a moment. "Come? Why not?"
"All right, Letta."
"At half past ten p.m. at the "Vinnichanka" restaurant. Opposite the entrance. That's it. I'm being waited for. Bye."
Short beeps. Khanya threw the receiver on the floor. He looked around tiredly. Money turned to ashes. Nurik. Letta and her wedding. Gosha, as it turned out, had disappeared again at such a crucial moment.

Leaving the front door unlocked, Khanya walked leisurely out of the house. Rakhit had opened the hood and was checking the oil level in the car.

"Yura, do you remember where the restaurant "Vinnichanka" is?"
"What? "Vinnichanka"? I've never heard of it. We should ask the guys. Are our enemies gathering there?"
"No, they're not. I asked just in case."

***

Both Nurik and Khanya were expecting an easy victory. One had accepted the role of the master of Kiev. The other had no doubt that it would be very easy to throw off his opponent. Both of them expected to succeed, but neither of them managed to do it at once. Moreover, they both reached an impasse, overestimating their own capabilities and underestimating their opponent. The conflict dragged on and grew, involving more and more forces. The opinions of the thieves were divided. Some of them supported Khanya, while others supported Nurik. Most of the bandits were waiting to see which side would be outnumbered and which would be stronger. Kiev's illegal business was paralyzed, currency transactions stopped, and hookers were afraid to go out on the streets. Taking advantage of the confusion, small gangs of teenagers began to terrorize the local population. The situation escalated against the backdrop of the looming economic crisis plaguing Ukraine. The introduction of the coupon system, another delusion of the Communists (who called themselves new-wave democrats), pushed Kiev toward even more chaos.

Nurik and Khanya realized that the guerrilla war could not last long. Someone had to retreat. Who? For now, both were suffering losses, taking occasional blows, thus wearing each other out.

Hasan had been shot in the chest, and Nurik had sent him to Moscow for treatment. Manyunya and Fatty ducked into the cellars like rats, directing the actions of their loyal bandits from there.

***

Gosha was busy. Korotyshka was helping him move things to his great aunt's apartment. Once, Gosha had already devoted himself to such a business - in anticipation of his first conviction. Then, the cops were sitting tight on his tail. A breeze of memories refreshed his brain, tickling his nerves pleasantly. Gosha hummed smugly:
"Khanya doesn't need to know what we do."
Korotyshka understood that.
Descending to the basement, Gosha bumped into Rakhit.
"What a light here. You could kill yourself," Gosha muttered instead of greeting him.
Khanya came out of the darkness from behind Rakhit. A smile lit up his face:
"Gosha, you've finally appeared! I didn't know what to think. Thank God, you're all right."
"Don't worry about me."
Small eyes from under wheaten eyebrows tried to see Khanya's face in the darkness as he climbed the stairs along the wall.
"How are the guys?"
"They've been up a little long. We'll get them off the chain one of these days."
"Yeah."
A glance into the darkness where the stairs began:
"How far are you going?"
"To get some air. You can ride with me."
Korotyshka wiped the sweat from his forehead, glancing at the shadows sliding down the walls toward the exit. They didn't say where they were going. Why. Might bump into someone unintentionally. Get into trouble. Khanya made the mess; let him

clean up his own mess. Korotyshka didn't like the prospect of an evening stroll in the company of the boss. He felt much calmer in the apartment with his friends.

***

The restaurant "Vinnichanka" was situated on the outskirts of the city, behind the Exhibition Centre, like a museum of past decades forgotten in time. It was far from being a place where they welcomed the new millennium or followed the latest trends in cooking.

The facade of the restaurant was like an archive of the Soviet times, which slowly deteriorated under the influence of time and nature. Horizontal strips of faded paint enveloped the facade, and the large windows, in which old velour curtains gleamed, seemed like a time loop that transported back in time. Two old vases with artificial flowers stood like guards in front of the entrance. Multicolored petals faded over time, but they remained witnesses of the era when these flowers were bright and colorful, and the restaurant "Vinnichanka" was a place for rendezvous and celebrations.

Above the front door hung a large poster with the inscription: "Vinnichanka Restaurant - your cozy corner of taste." In some sense, this inscription was true. The menu of "Vinnichanka" remained a temporary monument of that era, when prices were affordable, and the dishes, though not particularly exquisite, always brought joy and satisfaction. Here, one could order borshch like their grandmother cooked or dumplings that seemed forever imprinted on Soviet culinary culture.

Khanya smirked:

"How much do you have to disrespect a bride to celebrate a wedding in a place like that."

Gosha, sitting at the steering wheel, quipped:

"Not everyone has as much money as you do."

Khanya's bodyguard was smoking in the car nearby, sitting comfortably behind Rakhit's back.

Violetta walked out of the restaurant doors in a translucent wedding dress. A group of tipsy guests had gone outside for a smoke.

"I'm here," she said instead of greeting, peeping into the car through the half-covered door.

"Get in quickly."

Gosha started the engine.

"I'll be right there. I'll just put on my raincoat."

The girl ran back. Gosha was confused:

"Where is she going, Oleg?"

Khanya shrugged his shoulders.

"What coat? Yes, she's gone crazy! In a minute or two, all the guests would be near the car."

This time, the fragile figure appeared accompanied by her husband, who was a bodybuilder and Violetta's classmate. Khanya involuntarily admired Violetta's luxurious brown hair, which fell on the open back. She looked incredibly beautiful in her wedding dress.

Gosha's voice brought Khanya back to earth.

"I told you all the guests would gather. It won't be without a fight. Tell me what you want. Or don't we have enough problems?"

Violetta was talking to her husband, who was holding her wrists tight. Leaning forward, she set her lips to kiss him. Letting go of her wrists, the groom tried to put his arms around his wife. Deftly diving under his arms, the girl freed herself from the embrace of her tipsy husband and got into the car. Behind her, there were cries of surprised guests.

***

Nurik sat in a cramped room and smoked hashish. The herb penetrated every cell of his consciousness, breaking his perception into thousands of tiny fragments. The potion, brought from Vladikavkaz, gently tingled his imagination like a magic weave of feelings and illusions.

Nurik's mind was in terrible confusion. Memories of the past melted away, dreams became nightmares, and reality dissolved into chaos. Every moment was distorted, every thought torn to pieces and carried away by the current. The walls of the room seemed alive, moving back and forth, ready to crush him under their weight.

Outside, the windows were tightly closed, and only soft light penetrated the room, creating a sense of isolation from the outside world. Nurik was consumed by his visions, in which he became an observer of his own world. Time seemed infinite and multidimensional, and every second presented him with new visual and sound images.

Nurik could see colors that did not exist and hear sounds that the human ear could not pick up. His mind was completely absorbed in this dreamlike world where reality and fantasy became indistinguishable. Nurik was on the verge of boundless delight and frightening emptiness, and in this state, he sailed intoxicatingly on the boundless ocean of his consciousness.

At these moments everything that was happening around him, the whole struggle for power in Kiev seemed a meaningless game of red and white. Colors, sounds, and shapes were mixed in a world where reality lost its meaning.

Nurik looked at his hands as if they belonged to someone else and began to laugh. It was a very strange laughter, which sounded more like a shuddering, animalistic croak that tumbled uncontrollably out of his throat.

***

"Why did you do that?" Khanya hesitated to ask. The mute question hung in the silence.

"Don't judge me," Violetta said as if she had heard Khanya's reflection in the glass of the sideboard. – "Let me do as I please."

"Have I forbidden you anything?"

Hot breath pierced their bodies, entwined in languor. Rolling over the blanket in the faint glare of moonlight streaming through the half-drawn curtains, they kissed each other like mad, falling into the power of primal desire.

"How loudly your heart beats!" Khanya burst out, and only then did he realize that it was his own heart, trapped in the cramped chamber of his rib cage, that was tearing the skin from the inside out.

"Letta, I want you. I want every cell of your magical body...!"

"You have me," the girl whispered.

Sharp nails dug into Oleg's back. A drop of blood, sliding down his back, rolled to the floor to the clothes scattered in disorder, to the wedding dress. They were different as if they were from different worlds, but that was what they were alike in. Both he and she took pleasure in the pain they inflicted.

***

Traffic light. Red. Yellow. Green. Gosha cursed loudly when he saw that the old Moskvich in front of him did not move. "Either the starter is malfunctioning," thought Gosha, signaling the owner of "Moskvich," or the pensioner dozed off at the wheel." There was no way around it. For this purpose, it was necessary to back up, but a foreign car was waiting there.

Gosha leaned out the window, wanted to shout something, and ... suddenly faltered. A pair of sturdy guys in leather jackets came from the Moskvich and the jeep behind them. Only then, Gosha noticed that on the right there was Goloseevsky forest, on the left

- a deserted street, and there was no one, alas, no one on the deserted street, except for him and the two cars that blocked the traffic.

His hand, instinctively reaching for a cigarette, halfway down fell on the steering wheel. The wave of tension subsided, giving way to animal fear and.... relief. Gosha clearly realized that his fate was sealed, and before the car doors opened, before the body in the gray sweater was dragged out onto the sidewalk, he had already agreed to everything. For he had already lost.

***

"I have to go," a voice woke him up.

Khanya opened his eyes. Surprisingly, he hadn't slept so soundly and sweetly in a long time. There was not a single concern, not a single worry that could distort his sleep. It was a moment of total presence, a moment when past and future ceased to matter. Khanya didn't want to wake up.

The blinding, bright daylight hit his eyes painfully. A moment ago, their bodies had been lying close together, as if they were two parts of the same whole, and in that moment, there was nothing more important in the universe, and now...

"Are you leaving?"

Violetta hurriedly put on her stockings, tightly pressing her stubborn lips, swollen after a stormy night.

"Where are you going?"

Khanya watched the sunlight play on Violetta's hair, making it shine like gold.

"Don't ask stupid questions."

"Then why did you come?"

The girl rose sharply from the sofa.

"Get dressed quickly! Aren't you going to walk me out?"

Khanya threw a shirt over his shoulders:

"Still...?"

Violetta shrugged her shoulders:
"I wanted to see you one last time."
"Did you?"
"Yes."
"What next?"
"Nothing."
They left the house.
"I don't understand why you did that. Not before. Not later. On your wedding night."
"My husband deserved it."
"No man deserves to have his bride sleep with another man on their wedding day. No man! No matter what kind of man he is!"
Then, after a pause, he continued:
"You don't love him. Then why have you married him? Is it only because you must or it's time to? Or you wanted in such a way to hurt me?"
"Why don't you stop moralizing? You're a moralist!"
Violetta flared up.
Khanya was silent. He saw before him a completely different Violetta, the one he did not know.
"Don't hookers in wedding dresses who pretend to be virgins turn you on? Don't they?"
Violetta looked down at Khanya mockingly. Khanya flared up, barely restraining himself from hitting her.
The girl arrogantly said:
"At least now I'm fully secured financially. And independent! My husband has rich, influential parents."
Khanya smiled sadly, looking at her:
"Independent? From what and from whom? Look at you: you're like a child. With brains like yours, you should be playing with dolls and gaining life experience, not getting married."
A cab with a green light slowed down near them. Oleg opened the car door, pointing Violetta to the back seat.

"You..." Violetta took offense. - "I didn't think that we would part with you like this."

"We broke up a long time ago. Back in the spring. Have you forgotten that?"

Khanya remained standing in the street.

"Bye," Khanya waved goodbye. – "Happy marriage!"

Violetta got into a cab.

"Oleg!"

Khanya turned around. Violetta's eyes glistened with tears:

"Oleg, I love you."

Khanya defiantly and leisurely looked at his watch. Stuck his hands in his pockets. Raised his eyes at Violetta:

"I don't need such love."

***

Rakhit, breathing heavily after running up the stairs, sprang to the door behind which he had left the boss with the girl in the wedding dress yesterday. No one answered the tentative call. In desperation, Rakhit started pounding the door with his hands indiscriminately, to no avail. They had missed each other! Why? Why hadn't Khanya waited for him as they had agreed last night? Yura crouched on the top step, not knowing what to do next. He couldn't understand what was going on around him. Tonight, someone had sent Khanya's militants home. Now, they could all be killed in a matter of hours if they wanted to. Ahmed and Nurik's men had taken over the safe house, waiting for Khanya's possible arrival. Rakhit himself had miraculously survived. There's a reason, they say, he has a dog's sense of smell. If Rakhit hadn't left his car two blocks from the right place... If he hadn't seen it in time. If...

The fellow rubbed his temples frantically with his palms. Khanya was gone, and if he was, he was in danger, and ninety percent against ten that Nurik would not miss such prey.

Quiet footsteps interrupted Rakhit's musings. Khanya was slowly coming up the stairs, munching on a bun. Yura jumped up in surprise:
"Oleg! Where are you coming from?"
Khanya took the apartment keys out of his pocket.
"I put the girl in a cab and came back."
"It's good that you haven't left!"
"Haven't we agreed otherwise?"

***

Violetta stepped cautiously into the hallway as if trying to get home unnoticed. Her cloak was in her hands, which she quickly threw on the coat rack and gracefully took off her shoes.
Violetta walked into the kitchen, pulling a can of coffee from the cabinet. When her husband heard her footsteps, he, in a wrinkled suit, got up from the sofa and went to the kitchen. The door was left ajar.
"Where have you been?" His voice was trembling with anger.
"None of your business," Violetta said harshly.
"What do you mean? None of my business?"
The husband was confused. His face was flushed with rage. Violetta turned to him sharply:
"You got drunk at our wedding like an asshole. I was ashamed to sit next to you at the same table, let alone anything more! I called a friend, and her husband picked me up in his car. We cried all night sitting in the kitchen."
Tears splashed from her brown eyes. Violetta's husband tried to hug his wife, but she turned away.
"Viola, I'm sorry."
His hands slid down. The husband sank to his knees, hugging Violetta's legs.

"My darling, I didn't mean to hurt you. I'm sorry. It will never happen again," the husband repeated again and again, kissing his wife's delicate hands.

Violetta averted her eyes and indifferently watched the coffee brewing.

CHAPTER VI

"I advise you to leave."

Khanya shook his head.

"From Kiev? Never."

Rakhit twirled the car keys nervously in his hands.

"Kiev is a small city. It's not hard to find a man in it. We'll get killed."

Khanya was carefully wiping his revolver with an oiled cloth, stirring the sugar in his tea mug with a spoon from time to time.

"Maybe we will. Does it make a difference? Life doesn't deserve to be taken too seriously," then he added, looking curiously at the cartridges scattered on his palm: "Why should you worry? No one wants your life. They are looking for me."

Raлhit was offended by the words, "No one wants your life." He hesitated and asked again with concern:

"Do you think they won't touch me?"

"They will not kill you, but if they do, you will look as good as usual."

Rahit did not like the joke:

"You're such an asshole..."

"Does that surprise you?"

Khanya hid the revolver in the waistband of his pants.

"Shall we go?"

"Where to?"

Khanya shrugged indifferently:

"Does it matter? We can't stay here forever..."

***

A man with a soft and tired voice sat on the grass not far from the BMW. With his head back, Blond was enjoying the gentle rays of the autumn sun. The bright rays played in the foliage of the trees, coloring it in golden and red shades.
"You shouldn't have come. In Moscow, the climate is much healthier for the body."
Lord opened his eyes. Khanya was standing over him. Lord smiled a strange, barely perceptible smile, looking intently into Khanya's eyes.
"It's boring out there right now."
"We're having fun, though."
Lord stood up.
"Yes, I've heard."
"Where are we going?" Rakhit's voice came from behind him.
Blond did not move. He shifted his gaze leisurely to Rakhit.
"Go alone."
Blond stood up, shaking the dust off his knees.
"I suggest you walk more often. Oleg, if they find you, they'll find you by your car."

***

Nurik did not expect the protracted confrontation to be resolved so quickly after so many unsuccessful efforts. With one cunning, well-thought-out move, Nurik had solved all the problems. If not today, then tomorrow will supporters and opponents know about it. Now he, and only he, will dictate his will. It was not for nothing that Nurik was called a fox in the camps. A smile flashed across his pimply face.
Manyunya hasn't returned yet. He and Fatty are on the prowl around the city, wanting to get their revenge for Ahmed. It's a

foolish thing to do now. It's a waste of time. Khanya is hiding. It's hard to find out where he's hiding yet. We need to let time pass. Sooner or later, Khanya will show up. Besides, what can he alone do against Nurik?

Nurik's thoughts returned to Manyunya. He wondered whether all wrestlers had liquid mush instead of brains. But for him, for Nurik, it's not bad. Manyunya can't understand that there is no need to kill Khanya. It's much more profitable to put Khanya in his place for the edification of others.

***

Lord's girlfriend was in her last year of high school. The word "school" didn't really fit a seasoned hooker who'd been serving clients since she was twelve. Her appearance was designed to confuse the people around her. In some unfathomable way, she combined the beauty of an angel with the ruthlessness of a predator. Her blonde hair was so light that it seemed as if the rays of the sun lived in its strands. Waves of hair fell over her shoulders like gentle clouds tempting with their touch. She always wore it loose, and it made her look like an innocent doll, ready to fly away on its wings into the world of fairy tales. But she didn't believe in fairy tales and despised human weaknesses. The feelings of compassion and kindness were unknown to her.

Like Lord's, her eyes were as blue as bottomless lakes and as soft as morning mist. They sparkled brightly, like two sapphires, and there was something mysterious in them, inaccessible to understanding. But behind that innocent glaze lay coldness and burning emptiness.

Her skin was pure and snow-white, but beneath that whiteness pulsed a kind of animal strength unnatural to a human and capable of satisfying a pack of hungry males. Her figure was slender and graceful as if made for dancing under the moon. She always wore outfits that emphasized her femininity and availability. Her words were sharp as blades, and her smile was as sinister as a predator's. She rarely went to school. Today, however, she went to class, which seemed rather strange. Her mother was under compulsory treatment for alcoholism, and therefore, no one prevented a man with a soft and tired voice from feeling himself a full-fledged master in a half-empty apartment on those rare days when he happened to come to Kiev.

Taking his jacket off his shoulders and not finding a suitable hook in the hallway, Khanya took it into the room. He placed the jacket on the windowsill.

"I can't believe that Gosha is a traitor."

"I don't see anything strange about it," said Lord, putting his hands behind his head and stretching lazily on the chair. "I remember well who Gosha was in the camps and who he tried to pretend to be here. He decided he was being clever."

"How did it happen? You always know everything."

"What's not to know? I heard Gosha was pulled out of the car by Ahmed's men on the outskirts of the city. Nurik was wise. Gosha wasn't beaten or tortured. He was taken to the forest, where he witnessed a cheaply staged performance. A man was killed in front of Gosha: he was buried up to his neck in the ground, then his head was blown off with a scythe. Then, they chopped the victim into small pieces with an axe. After that, Gosha was offered either to go to a better world or to leave the game and take the maximum number of your supporters out of it, which he successfully did. And our mutual friend has a moral justification. He did not go over to their side but took a neutral position. That's one. He saved his life. That's two. In addition, his favorite car, which, by the way, they promised to burn, remained unharmed. That's three. True, in doing so," the soft and tired voice laughed, "he sacrificed you. But that's kind of operating expense, so don't be angry."

"I can imagine how Nurik thanked that scavenger afterwards."

Lord reached for a bottle of "Borjomi".
"You can't imagine. Gosha was not touched. Why? Nurik's bandits will have you to punish Gosha for what he has done."
Khanya smiled bitterly:
"It seems so."
Looking out the window:
"You know quite a lot. A stranger among strangers?"
"Maybe..."
"Who did they kill in front of Gosha?"
"A homeless man begging at the train station. They washed him, cut his hair, dressed him up. They told him to pretend to be the director of some mythical company and to answer "no" to all questions when they started demanding money from him in front of Gosha. Then Nurik's men pretended to beat him up, and he agreed and begged for mercy. They promised the homeless man a hundred rubles for his service and a bottle of vodka in addition if he played the specified role properly. So, he played his role and went to a better world. They do that quite often nowadays when they want to intimidate."
"I don't think Gosha would believe it."
Lord smirked:
"It's hard not to believe when they kill a man in front of you and cut the body into small pieces. For today, you are alone. Those who could have fought on your side were discouraged by Gosha. Don't forget that thieves are either on your side or against you."
"Rakhit wasn't afraid."
"What's the use of him? He can't do anything else but drive a car. Let the boy go. Don't drag him to the grave. Let him live."
Khanya raised his left eyebrow:
"What about me? What? Am I not going to live anymore?"
"Not me, but us," Blond replied quietly. "Not everything is as bad as it may seem at first glance. You lost a lot, but not everything. You didn't chicken out. You didn't compromise. That's a lot, but it

takes a deed to regain respect and power. A bold move! Perhaps it's time to meet the men who've been looking for you so hard. It's just a shame we have to warn them in advance. And we won't have a very pleasant conversation with them. Well, that's all right. We'll go together."
Khanya looked gratefully at Blond.
"Thank you. I've always believed in you."
"You shouldn't," Lord smiled. "You should only believe in yourself. Trusting others is sheer folly."
Then he repeated it in a low voice as if remembering something that had happened a long, long time ago:
"Only in yourself."

***

Manyunya studied Fatty's sweaty face incredulously:
"There's obviously some kind of trick here."
"I don't think so," Nurik said, puffing on his cigarette. "Khanya has no other way. He can't fight. Run away? Greed won't let him go. He'll probably ask me to keep him autonomous, working under our control, so he can stab us in the back when we let our guard down. It would sound reasonable and financially mutually beneficial."
Manyunya's translucent eyes nearly popped out of their orbits.
"Is that something you're willing to agree to? You are ..."
"What am I?" Nurik said sharply. He affectionately patted the wrestler on the cheek. "It's not good to raise your voice at your elders. Didn't they teach you ethical behavior as a child?"
Manyunya crumpled, gloomily fixed a sullen look at the bridge of Nurmagomedov's nose.
"That's better."
Nurik's swollen face broke into a smile.
"And Khanya?"

"I'll give him to you. Do whatever you want with him," he sighed. "As you can see I'd do anything for my friend."

***

Lord came to pick up Khanya with a bearded, stoutly built man of oriental type.
"Who is this?" Khanya half-questioned, watching the stranger's measured movements as he poured a can of gasoline into the tank of Zhiguli.
"Jafar. A good guy. He stole a car especially for us so we wouldn't have to walk to Nurik. Everyone in Georgia knows him. He served 15 years for banditry. He was in the camps with Ioseliani."
"That name sounds familiar."
"You've got to be kidding me!" Blond was genuinely surprised. "People like Dzhaba Ioseliani are the foundation of the world."
The stranger slammed the trunk:
"One thing I can say is that it won't stall on the road," then looked intently into the blue eyes and asked, "If Dyuba asks, when will you be in Tbilisi?"
"Someday I will..."
Lord sat at the wheel. The car started slowly. Khanya looked back at Jafar. An interesting man. Came from nowhere and went away to nowhere.

***

They were expected. Several dozen cars surrounded a vacant lot on the outskirts of the city. Lord pulled off the road toward the vacant lot. Stopped.
"It is a cheerless place."
The figures of people who had been strolling leisurely along the vacant lot turned toward the car as if on cue. At this distance, Khanya could only guess who was who by their clothes. White blurred faces that radiated distrust and hostility.

"Why did you come with me?" Khanya didn't recognize his own voice. "You know as well as I do that we were not and never will be friends. The only thing we had in common was money. Nothing else..."

Lord smiled mockingly:

"It turns out you know how to be sincere."

"Am I wrong?"

"No, you are not."

Blond kept his eyes on the long row of cars.

"You're shit. I don't know if you're better than me or worse. Out there in that clearing there is the logical conclusion of your biography. Or the beginning of a career. As luck would have it. - After a moment's silence, he continued in an indifferent tone: - Why? We wear the same suit. You think in the same terms as I do. You look at the world from the corner of the prison cell where I am destined to be, too. All people are divided by the bars. Some ignore it. Others bang their foreheads against the steel bars every day. We stand next to each other, not opposite each other. Am I making myself clear enough?"

"Roughly, yes."

Lord rubbed the bridge of his nose with the pads of his index finger and thumb.

"Part of the reason I came with you is for the money. In case of success I'm in business. And, generally, for boredom. Life is such nonsense that if you don't cheer yourself up once in a while, you'll burn out in a drug-induced white fever. So, are we going, or have you changed your mind?"

"Let's go. We can't deny them the pleasure..."

Zhiguli, gaining speed, drove into the vacant lot.

***

"Nurik, it's them!"

Manyunya squinted his left eye and stared tensely in the direction of the approaching car. The sun's glare playing on the windshield created a flickering noise that made it hard to see the faces sitting in the car. Manyunya felt the hot light blinding him, making him blink and squint again.
"They are," Nurik hissed.
"I don't see who Khanya's driver is."
"A new car gets a new driver," Fatty said with a judicious snicker.

***

Lord stopped the car a few steps away from Nurik and Manyunya, driving into the crowd so that there was open space behind the car.
"Are you ready?" Lord's body resembled a spring, elastically compressed before a throw.
"Yes."
"Remember, Oleg, we have exactly nine seconds."
Lord lit the safety fuse protruding from under the seat.
"Let's go!"
The crowd around the car recoiled as Lord and Khanya jumped out of the car with revolvers. Nurik moved stealthily behind Fatty.
"One."
No one realized why the arrivals rushed out. Why was Khanya fleeing so quickly from the meeting place if he had dared to come to it? Why did they need guns if they hadn't fired a single shot from them?
"Two."
Khanya had never run so fast before. It was a speed he had never felt before - a speed that suddenly became the most important thing to him. His heart was beating so hard it seemed ready to burst out of his chest, and even his breath was trying to catch up with his legs.

"Just as long as no one blocks the road, no one stops!" was the only thought that pulsed the blood in his temples. His whole life, like a spring, compressed and concentrated into that one moment.
"Three."
- Where are they going, huh? - Manyunya looked at Nurik over his shoulder confusedly.
"Four."
Blond suddenly remembered how he had chased a pigeon across the playground when he was two or three. It seemed like he was about to grab the bird by the wings. The pigeon soared into the sky and flew away. The little boy cried loudly out of resentment, and it took a long time to calm him down.
"Five."
Khanya felt the tart pain squeeze his lungs, the lack of air and strength. Multicolored circles swam before his eyes, bright highlights.
"Six."
"Get them!" Whose shout was that? Several teenagers, eager to show off in front of Nurik, rushed after them.
"Seven."
Nurik looked inside Zhiguli. A grimace of fear contorted the pimply face in a grin. "Get back!"
"Eight."
"Jump!"
"Your voice hasn't changed even now. Thank you, Lord, I know how to count." Khanya pressed himself into the damp earth with his whole body as if begging: "Hide me. Take me into your bosom. Shelter me. Keep me safe."
"Nine."
A tremendous explosion deafened his eardrums with pain. An avalanche of dirt, rock, metal, and earth rained down on the prostrate body. His shirt was soaked. From sweat? From blood?

Khanya jumped up. The collarbone of his left arm was numb with pain. Without aiming, he fired into the panic-stricken crowd, into the cars engulfed in flames, and into the people terrified with fear and pain. Some fell. Some squirmed, trying to get up. Blind, randomly fired bullets sliced the air above their heads in response. Dragging his legs, Khanya staggered toward the center of the clearing, firing his revolver at everyone. In the chaos of the explosion, no one paid any attention to him, and that surprised him.

Lord was lying on his side. Blood was gushing from his throat and his shrapnel-strewn abdomen. Intestines, mixed with slime of a dirty brown color, spilled out. "Cretins," he breathed out, his lips turning white, his eyes glassy as he looked to the heavens.

***

Barred windows. A hunched investigator was poring over papers in a narrow room at a cheap government desk. Opposite him, by a huge metal safe, sat a calm young man in a strict business suit.

"I don't know what they have blown up there, captain. As you know, there were two of us, and there were three hundred of them with knives, chains, and, as you found out, firearms."

"So, you go on saying you had nothing to do with what happened?"

"Absolutely."

"There are witnesses."

"From the people who came there to kill us? Their testimony can't be objective, and they're the only ones you have."

Squinting his eyes, the investigator glared at the person under investigation. He patted the palm of his hand on the weighty folder.

"There's enough material in here to put you behind bars for at least ten years."

Khanya shrugged skeptically.

"Is that a threat?"

"It's a reality."

Khanya laughed in the detective's face. There was a note of contempt in his voice. This detective looked not much different from the other law enforcement officers whom Khanya paid salary. And the way he spoke, he was just like all of them - corrupt and greedy.

"I advise you think about whether you need it actually," Khanya said quietly, licking the dry corners of his mouth with the tip of his tongue. "Anyway, your scrupulous attitude to the service will change absolutely nothing."

EPILOGUE

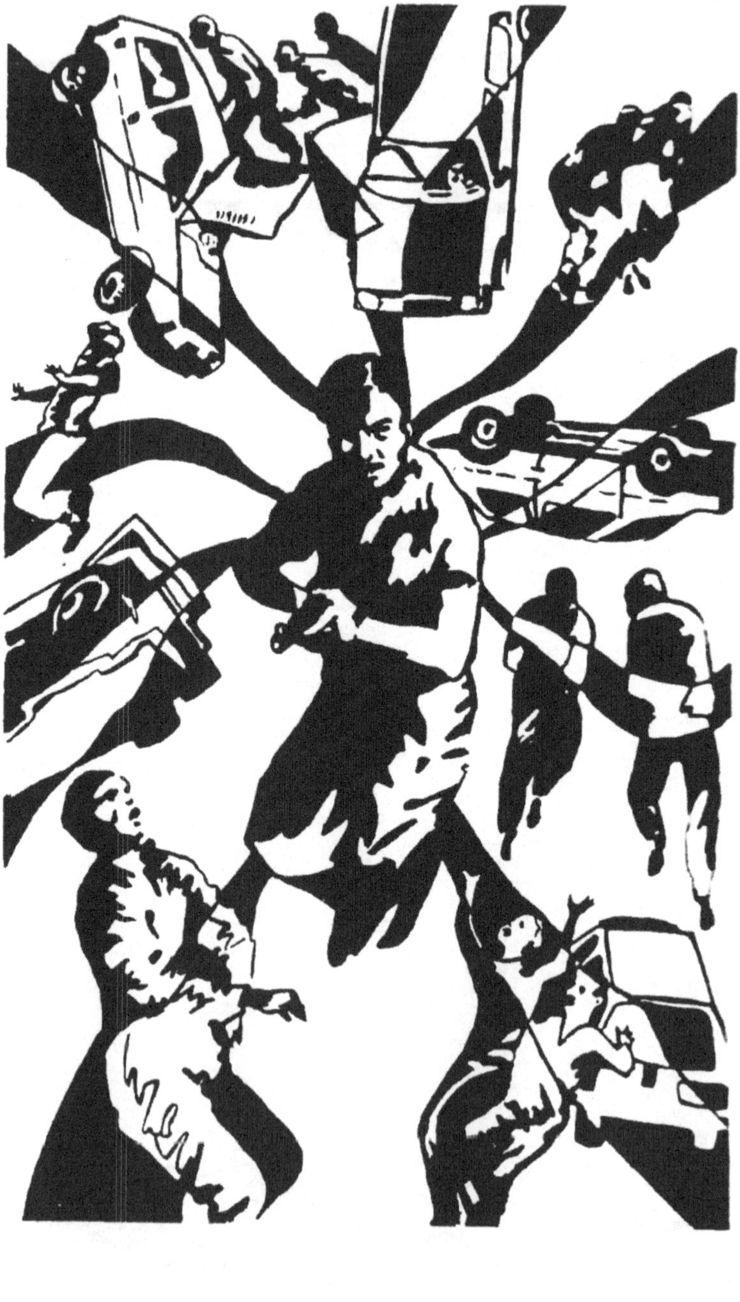

It took Khanya a month and a half to eliminate his rivals and regain his power. By December 1990, he had established control over Kiev's shadow economy. Based on scattered gangs, Khanya created a powerful structure that divided Kiev into spheres of influence. Over the next two years, Khanya was brought to criminal responsibility three times. He was not convicted, however. There were five attempts on his life. Miraculously did he slip out of the clutches of death. On April 7, 1992, at 7:45 a.m. on a Kiev-New York flight, he emigrated under a false name to the United States. Where he is now and what he is up to generally is unknown.

* * *

On February 10, 1991, the half-decomposed corpse of a tall man wearing a coarse-knit gray sweater was found in a wooded area near the Odessa highway in the direction of Vasilkov. The crime remained unsolved.

* * *

On December 1, 1991, Ukraine gained its independence. The USSR had crumbled into a multitude of states. The great empire, which occupied one-sixth of the land, ceased to exist. Freedom and independence - these beautiful words remained words. In reality, the collapse of the USSR created chaos and numerous bloody conflicts between and within the former republics of the USSR.

* * *

Viktor Nikiforov, known as Kalina, was killed in Moscow at the age of 28 by two shots to the back of his head. It happened in the late evening of January 14, 1992, at the entrance to his house on

Yeniseyskaya Street, when he was returning home with his wife. He was buried in the Vostryakovskoye cemetery.

It was rumored that on the eve of his death, Kalina killed the Luberet's authority, Mansur Shelkovnikov, during a quarrel. In response, people close to Mansur hired a hitman. However, in the opinion of many, it was not revenge but a kind of solution to the personnel issue. Kalina was Mansur's successor, but his candidacy did not suit the criminal world.

Officially, the murder of Viktor Nikiforov remained unsolved.

* * *

A hooker who bore a striking resemblance to Karina, Ahmed's former girlfriend, was found in a sewer in a Budapest suburb in July 1992. Because the body had been mutilated as if it had been put through a meat grinder, no definitive identification could be made.

* * *

In July 1995, Violetta gave birth to a daughter. Five years later, she divorced her husband and never remarried. She worked for a construction company and then as a cashier in a supermarket.

* * *

Vladimir Baranovsky became an inveterate drunkard. In the early 2000s, he worked part-time as a loader in a grocery store near Leo Tolstoy Square. It was his only relatively stable job. He was fired for drinking and fighting with his coworkers. He got by on odd jobs. All the money was spent on vodka. He died in poverty on March 38, 2009. His body was found near the entrance to the house where he lived.

* * *

Pleshyvyi suddenly withdrew into the shadows and then reappeared in another capacity, joining the board of directors of Mercury, a manufacturing and commercial firm engaged primarily in intermediary and trade and procurement operations. After the firm was closed and criminal proceedings were instituted against its founders, he fled to Israel.

* * *

Rakhit was killed in a car accident.

* * *

Lord's girlfriend successfully married a well-known Ukrainian politician and turned into a successful, respectable businesswoman. She died of a drug overdose at the age of 36.

* * *

Doctor of Philology Jaba Konstantinovich Ioseliani, professor of the Georgian State Institute of Theater and Cinema, author of over 100 publications, three monographs, four novels, and six plays.
He is also a criminal authority and code-bound thief, nicknamed Dyuba, who served more than 25 years in prisons and camps, the leader of the armed formation "Mkhedrioni," the backbone of which were former prisoners, drug addicts, and criminals of all stripes. In the early eighties of the last century, Jaba Ioseliani initiated the reform of the criminal world of the USSR, which led to merging of the criminal world with the official bodies.
On February 27, 2003, Jaba Ioseliani suddenly felt ill. An ambulance took him to the Republican Hospital of Tbilisi, where doctors diagnosed a stroke and performed a neurosurgical operation. On March 4, 2003, Jaba Iosseliani died without regaining consciousness. He is buried in the Didubi Pantheon of Writers and Public Figures of Georgia.

* * *

Khanya's empire didn't last long. Too many people wanted money, power, and recognition. The carefully thought-out structure collapsed into small groups like a house of cards, often run by complete freaks or morons. More or less intelligent heads pumped the illegally gained money into the legal business and gradually withdrew from criminal affairs while retaining their influence in the criminal environment.

* * *

A full-figured, flabby-faced man of indeterminate age, with his head cocked high, got out of a Mercedes. A massive platinum ring framed with diamonds glittered on the ring finger of his right hand. The doormen stepped aside respectfully. The man was familiar to them. He was one of those who liked to say, "I am the boss in this city." Looking at the rough rat-like features of his face, it was not that simple to recognize Korotyshka, who used to sell lingerie in his youth.

CONTENTS

ABOUT THE BOOK
"THE BLACK SUIT"   ....   page 3

PART I   5
CHAPTER I   7
CHAPTER II   21
CHAPTER III   31
CHAPTER IV   44
CHAPTER V   56
CHAPTER VI   71

PART II   85
CHAPTER I   87
CHAPTER II   100
CHAPTER III   110
CHAPTER IV   122
CHAPTER V   135
CHAPTER VI   143

PART III	....	155
CHAPTER I	....	157
CHAPTER II	....	169
CHAPTER III	....	179
CHAPTER IV	....	190
CHAPTER V	....	203
CHAPTER VI	....	217
EPILOGUE	....	229

Made in the USA
Las Vegas, NV
17 February 2024